When Cicadas Sing

When Cicadas Sing

John A Burgess

ISBN:	Hardcover	978-1-6641-0749-6
	Softcover	978-1-6641-0748-9
	eBook	978-1-6641-0747-2

Print information available on the last page.

Rev. date: 01/31/2022

To order additional copies of this book, contact:
Xlibris
NZ TFN: 0800 008 756 (Toll Free inside the NZ)
NZ Local: 9-801 1905 (+64 9801 1905 from outside New Zealand)
www.Xlibris.co.nz
Orders@Xlibris.co.nz
837206

Contents

Dedicated to our dearly loved son, Gregory Shaun Burgess, who never got to read this tale centred on the Armstrong family holiday property
He described Ōmahanui on Clendon Point as his spiritual home, greatly enjoying time there for forty-six years without exception, from being a bump in his mother's tummy until his untimely death at the age of 48.

Acknowledgements

Special thanks to
Michael Gifford (80) and Elise Vacherand (14) for their helpful evaluation of the manuscript
Faye Adams for drawing the illustrative map
Our grandchildren for their enthusiastic interest and support
And particularly my wife, Robyn, who so frequently accepted my absent-minded replies whilst I wrote or edited. 'She is worth far more than rubies.' (Prov. 31:10)

Resemblance to any existing person may be intentional, but only those who know will recognise themselves despite the licence given to a work of fiction. The author sincerely apologises for any perception of offence. Such offence is entirely unintentional.

The bach,
the bay,
the place we feel at home.
Where the sound of waves against the shore
is our alarm clock and our lullaby,
and the cool bush envelops our one-room haven like a soft green hug.
The small feet of four generations have pitter-pattered on the same floor,
trekking sand and dirt throughout the ages.
Our friendly beach castle becomes a fortress at night,
sealing out nightmares like bogeymen and possums.
Sticky bodies in sleeping bags squeezed into bunks
that were always a touch too small,
toe to toe and feet on the roof, leaning against the wall to keep cool.
Squashed mozzies and bug spray on licked fingers;
whispering behind the curtain that swishes along the rail at ten past nine
while the adults talk in a grown-up whisper
and the chink of light in your eyes
keeps you up no matter how many times they say,
'Be quiet!'
Familiar sights, like life jackets hanging in mismatched uniform
and the rusty nail that sticks out below the
mirror, are always there to greet you,
as expected as the musty freshness of the room
when you first walk in
and the saltiness after a swim.
Crusty eyebrows and grubby toes, scratched bug-bites and the feeling of
never quite being clean may sound repulsive to some!
But they're **our** crusty eyebrows and they're **our** bitten legs
and when you laugh on the beach and spit oysters into the sand
you know that this is your home.
It belongs to us: four generations of feet.
And when the Jenga tiles hit the table with a crash and everybody cheers
we all know we're the luckiest people in the world.

Daya Czepanski

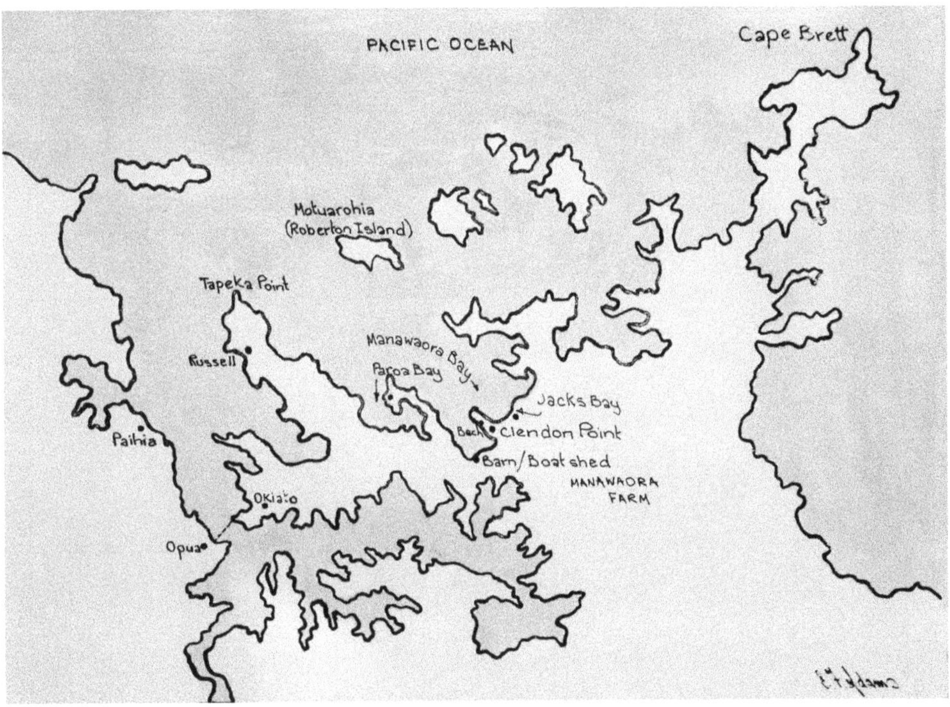
PACIFIC OCEAN
Cape Brett
Motuarohia
(Roberton Island)
Tapeka Point
Russell
Manawaora Bay
Paroa Bay
Jacks Bay
Bach
Clendon Point
Barn/Boat shed
MANAWAORA
FARM
Paihia
Okiato
Opua

FOREWORD

In New Zealand, the new school year starts in the last week of January, or sometimes the first week in February. After six or more weeks of summer holidays I have mixed feelings about returning to school. I really look forward to seeing my school friends again and hearing what they did and where they went. But it also marks the gradual end of summer daylight hours and free time, the start of homework at night and the extra stress of getting assignments handed in on time.

I returned for my second year at high school in 2008. On that first morning, my mum drove me to school and dropped me off near the school entrance before going to the hospital. As I walked towards the gate, looking for a face I recognised, a peculiar movement of bobbing heads appeared and then disappeared. I thought it strange, but I was completely unprepared for what happened next. All of a sudden, I was surrounded by a screaming melee of my friends and some hangers-on. I glimpsed a few boys grinning and clapping in the background. Someone had prepared a banner that jiggled up and down. It said, **'ALEX—OUR HERO. GIRLS CAN DO ANYTHING!!'**

I hadn't reckoned on a reception like this. I had a sneaking feeling I would be interrogated by my close friends about the events that happened between Christmas Day and New Year's Eve, but this was overwhelming. The excitement continued down the pathway and into the student courtyard. New kids stared, wondering what the fuss was about. Eventually, I was made to sit on a bench, and there was a lot of hushing as Nicole motioned for silence.

When everyone had settled down Nicole said, 'Alex, we are all dying to hear what really happened. Some of us read things in the New Zealand Herald, and saw your interview on TV, but we want to hear every single detail, don't we, girls?'

The expectant look on their faces and nodding of heads by some boys in the background meant I had to begin the story. There are so many intriguing and terrifying details to describe, it was impossible to tell 'every single detail'. That is why I have accepted my grandpa's offer to write it in a book with all the things I can remember and what he has learned through interviews with others who were involved.

I hope you enjoy reading it as much as I have.

Alex

Chapter 1

North

Alex loved going to the Bay of Islands. Their private beach on a bush-clad point jutting into the Bay of Islands was immense fun, but getting there on a public holiday seemed to take forever. If they could leave Auckland early enough to avoid the endless line of traffic that crawled like multicoloured snails through towns like Orewa and Wellsford, it might take just a little more than three hours. That wasn't so bad.

But it was Boxing Day, and they had left home mid-morning. Her mother had insisted upon making the house tidy following the pandemonium and excitement of Christmas Day, because she said it made coming home more pleasant. Alex couldn't see the point of tidying the house when no one would see it. Dad had muttered similarly.

'I can't bear coming home nicely relaxed after three weeks in the Bay of Islands only to have to start cleaning up,' she had responded. 'Now everyone help, please, and it shouldn't take too long.' The clipped tones of charge nurse Fionna Armstrong left no room for argument.

Samuel had taken the risk of playing with some of the Christmas presents neatly stored in his wardrobe. A shrill cry from Mum, some strong words from Dad, and tears from Samuel contributed to the tense atmosphere in their car as it finally accelerated from their house faster than usual. Alex saw Mum glance at Dad, who appeared not to notice, although she sensed a message had passed between them.

Quite soon they had joined the motorway traffic. 'Look at all those boats ahead!' Dad groaned. His tone suggested, *If we'd got away earlier, we wouldn't have all this nonsense.*

Detective Gregory Armstrong hated trailer boats in holiday traffic. They slowed everyone down, encouraging frustrated drivers to make risky passing manoeuvres. Then he would yell advice at them as if they could hear him. Alex found it amusing.

'There's nine,' offered Samuel. Samuel was quick with numbers.

'Never mind,' said Mum in a falsely bright voice. 'We'll probably get past them before we get to the hills. Dad's a smart driver.'

Fionna gave Greg's knee a light squeeze and left her hand there. Greg gave a grunt and pulled into the passing lane. A twin-axle trailer carrying an impressive boat and a huge outboard motor slid behind them, the car's driver leaning forward over his steering wheel in an effort to make his roaring motor go faster.

'One down,' said Greg.

'Eight to go,' Samuel drawled.

'Ten,' Greg countered. 'I've just seen two more ahead.' Fionna withdrew her hand from his knee.

There had followed a succession of boats and motor homes before the motorway came to an end. The main road north now offered one lane in each direction with occasional passing lanes. At times, trailers stacked high with holiday trappings and covered by fluttering tarpaulins slowed their progress to a crawl until a passing lane offered a chance to overtake. It seemed like everyone was leaving Auckland for holidays in the north, but once they had endured the three-kilometre snail-paced crawl through Wellsford, where two highways merged, the traffic gained speed.

'Two hours twelve to get to Wellsford,' fumed Greg.

Fionna selected a CD, and soon the car was filled with music. 'Loud enough?' she asked. Then, satisfied that everyone was happy, she removed her glasses, closed her eyes, and almost immediately began to sleep. Greg took a sideways look at her, then turning his head further, he winked back at Alex. Placing his left hand against his cheek and putting his head to the side he indicated she was asleep. Alex smiled and nodded at her father's eyes in the rear-vision mirror. She turned to pass the message on to her brother, but Samuel's eyes were closed and his head moved loosely with the motion of the car.

Samuel had the same fair hair as his sister, but he was fuller in the face and his freckled nose was smaller. He was probably going to look more like his father. Her father was handsome, and Alex was proud of him. She enjoyed reminding her friends that he was a detective at Auckland Central Police Station. These days, he wore clothes like a businessman, but Alex preferred him in his police uniform. Fionna thought Samuel looked a lot like his father also.

'Look at those two,' Fionna had smiled as the family ambled along the beach in Fiji earlier that year. 'Talk about a chip off the old block. Look at how he walks—just like his father.' Later, she had mentioned this to Greg, who seemed pleased.

'And what about Alexandra?' he had queried. 'Who does she look like?'

He had then teased Alex about resembling some of her less-attractive relatives before drawing her close and whispering, 'You are beautiful, just like your mother. What do you reckon?'

Alex had felt a warm glow. Mum was very pretty. When she had walked around the pool at the resort, Alex had noticed admiring looks following her.

At times, Alex worried about her own looks. She thought her nose was a bit pointy, and she had a smattering of freckles on her cheeks that made her seem younger than her 14 years. Although her eyes were more blue than hazel, they weren't a definite colour. She wished they were. Her fair hair hung halfway down her back and was usually tied back in a ponytail or sometimes plaited for a change. In Fiji, it had been skilfully woven with tight braiding and beads. She wore it for almost two months until Mum insisted on it being undone so it could be properly washed.

The smooth motion of the car had put her in that relaxed state halfway between waking and sleeping. In her dream, she was flying back from Fiji with the air rushing by and the dull roar of the jet engines pushing the plane through the perfectly clear sky.

The seat belt signal sounded and kept sounding. Alex found it annoying. She heard her mother say, 'Close the door, Greg.'

What? Has Dad opened the door? In mid-air? Everyone will get sucked out! In panic, Alex thrust her arms forward to grip the seat in front, while the signal continued to sound. She forced her eyes open, struggling to orientate herself. The cabin had seats just like Dad's car, and she could see a steering wheel. Where was the pilot? A shadow approached, and a door closed. Immediately the signal stopped.

'Sorry,' Greg said through the window, 'I should have removed the key.'

Alex's heart was racing. Her mother's face appeared around the seat. 'Well, haven't you had a good long sleep,' she said. 'You missed Whangārei and Kawakawa. Dad's checking to see how far away the ferry is,' she added.

'Are we at Ōpua already?' her sleep-thickened voice exclaimed.

'Yes,' replied Mum, 'already.'

'"Already" means four hours and twenty-three minutes.' Dad spoke through the open window. 'It's all right for some to sleep.' He looked with mock severity at Alex.

A mobile home, groaning off the ferry ramp in low gear, trailed diesel fumes as it turned along the small strip of waterfront shops. A continuous stream of cars, trucks, and trailer boats followed. Dad slid in behind the steering wheel and started the engine. The rear door burst open, and Samuel dived into the car.

'We're nearly there, Dad, aren't we,' stated Samuel, his voice shrill with excitement.

'Nearly there. About fifteen minutes after we get off the ferry. Unless we get behind some more slow traffic, that is.' His eyes caught Fionna's and they exchanged brief smiles.

The queue of vehicles began to move forward, and their station wagon rolled down the steel ramp and onto the vehicular ferry. The deep throb of diesel engines rose from below. Shortly, the engines revved as the pilot urged the boat, now heavily weighed down by its load, to break free from the concrete ramp. People gathered in groups beside the rails, the wind gently tousling their hair.

'May we get out, Dad?' Samuel implored.

'Is that OK with you, Mum?' Greg asked.

Her smile was sufficient for brother and sister to leave their seats in an instant. Alex stretched her cramped limbs and let the sea breeze blow her hair into loose tangles.

'Are you excited, Alex?' asked Samuel. ''Cause I am. When I get there, I'm going to go straight down to the beach and go around the rocks and find some of those really big crabs.' His eyes widened to emphasise how big the crabs would be.

'I think you should help carry gear from the car first, Samuel,' said Alex, sounding a little grown-up. 'Remember it's Mum's and Dad's holiday too.'

'That's very mature of you.' Greg's voice startled them both. 'You really are growing up.'

He leaned against the rail and gazed at the array of boats moored towards the shore.

'Which boat will we have, Sam?' asked Greg.

The two then discussed this topic of mutual interest while Alex sought out that house above the approaching cliff face. Last year, her father had pointed it out as he told her the story about Mr Asia, the drug baron who had built his house above the modest cliffs not far from the approaching jetty. She imagined him digging a secret tunnel from his house down to a hidden entrance just above the high-water mark. He was very clever at smuggling drugs into the country. Apparently, under cover of night, waterproof packages with radio locator beacons attached were dropped in the bay by yachts coming from Australia or Fiji. They were picked up by a high-speed power boat that brought them to the small sandy beach where a secret tunnel must have led up into the house that she saw clearly now. Dad was about her age when it happened, but Alex was certain that if it was happening right now, he would be on the case. What's more, she imagined he would be the one to solve the case and lock away the baddies for good. She felt extra safe with Dad around.

The diesel engines suddenly died, and Alex left her imaginings at the railing as she followed Dad and Samuel back to their holiday laden station wagon. After a few throbs and thrusts from the engines and a gentle nudge against the oyster-encrusted piles, the forward motion ceased, and the steel ramp began to lower. Doors slammed and motors started as vehicles prepared to drive off the ferry.

Alex hadn't noticed before, but to her left was a very dusty and battered vehicle. As she gazed idly at it, her eyes met those of a Māori boy looking directly at her. The moment her eyes met his, he turned away, pretending he hadn't been looking. Alex was still taking in his handsome profile when he looked back. She had just raised her hand to give him a friendly wave, when the window was filled with two huge white eyes, a wide open mouth, and a long pink tongue thrust outwards and down. Her hand went instinctively to her mouth to smother the scream that started just as Greg accelerated away and down the ramp. As Alex glanced back, she imagined she saw white teeth framed by a laughing mouth.

'Is everything all right, you two?' Greg's eyes looked at Alex from the rear-vision mirror.

'Yes,' blurted Samuel. 'Alex just got excited.' Alex didn't know quite how to answer.

'Alex?' Greg's eyes questioned her from the mirror.

'Yes,' she managed, then added, 'A Māori boy just did that haka thing out his window. It gave me a fright.'

'A Māori boy?' Fionna inquired.

'In that old bomb.' Alex swivelled her head to indicate the vehicle that had moved in behind. Dad stared in the rear-vision mirror.

'The one that's keeping right on our tail,' he said. 'We'll soon get rid of him.'

The station wagon urged forward with a growl up the twisting road from the jetty. But there was no passing the two slower cars in front, and almost immediately, the wagon slowed again. Alex twisted in her seat belt and strained her head above the jumble of items piled almost to the roof behind her seat. Dad had left just enough gap for his rear-vision, and after several attempts, she saw the large head of a bearded driver.

A bare elbow hung out the driver's window, and brown shoulders stretching a dark singlet almost filled the windscreen. His hand wedged an upright cigarette on the steering wheel. Beside him, the head of a small woman peered over the dashboard, a knitted pink hat pulled towards a nose that drew comically close to her chin. Between the two, leaning forward from the rear seat, Alex spotted the white-toothed grin of the boy. As the road offered little opportunity for passing, the cars travelled several kilometres in single file.

Alex noticed her father glancing from rear mirror to side mirror and back. On the brow of an incline, his shoulders tightened and his hands grasped the steering wheel more firmly. In a low voice, he said, 'Don't be a silly beggar.'

'I'm not doing anything!' Samuel protested.

'Not you, Sam,' Greg replied. 'It's that stupid driver behind. If he's not careful, he'll drive right up my exhaust!'

This thought greatly amused Samuel. He started to say something, but the words were cut short by the bellicose roar of a high-revving motor, as a pink hat slid by, followed by whites of eyes above an enormous tongue in the rear side window. Greg stabbed hard on the brakes as the passing vehicle dived into the small gap in front. An approaching car flashed past, the crescendo of its horn vanishing instantly with it. Everyone lurched forward. Alex's heart raced, and the colour drained from her face.

'Idiot!' Greg bellowed. 'Can you believe what he just did?'

'Get his number and report him, Dad,' Samuel squeaked.

Alex noted her mother's face in profile, blotched red from throat to cheek. 'Just back off, Greg,' she demanded. 'Don't antagonise him. We don't want extra problems with Māoris.' The offending car filled their windscreen.

'Now you can drive up *his* exhaust, Dad,' Samuel urged.

Greg grunted. 'I'll more than do that. I'll run him off the road.' Then as Fionna's head snapped around, he hastily explained that this would be the work of the law, not deliberate collision.

The Māori boy's face appeared at the rear window. Cheerfulness and impertinence were together etched on his grinning face. Greg was not amused.

'Cheeky young sod. I'd like to wipe that smile off his face.'

Despite the fright he had given her and his rudeness, Alex was beginning to find it all quite amusing. Perhaps it was her parents' reaction. Adults can act strangely with kids who don't fear adults or consequences. Alex wondered if this boy would be quite so impertinent if he was face to face with her detective dad. Probably not.

The face disappeared as the car swung out abruptly. A raucous bellow and belch of white smoke burst from its exhaust as it sped past a line of cars. A reaction of red brake lights lit as, one after the other, cars hastily pulled aside.

'Just leave it, Greg.' Fionna's voice was as firm as a schoolteacher's final warning.

'It's all right. I wasn't going to go after him,' he assured her as he leaned his head towards the side window. 'He's made it,' he announced, 'but they're headed for trouble, just you wait and see.'

Silence filled the station wagon. Alex pictured them rounding a corner and finding that car slammed into a clay bank, with bodies slumped against blood-spattered windows and steam spewing from its engine.

Soon their indicators blinked for the turn-off that would take them to Ōmahanui. Most traffic continued on to Russell, so the pace quickened despite the winding road. This road had always seemed endless when Alex was younger, especially when it was a gravel surface. Now it was sealed and she was older, so the next minutes were a time of mounting anticipation.

Rounding a tight bend, Greg braked sharply and swerved to avoid a car wedged against a fern-covered bank and the edge of the road. In one moment, Alex took in the scene. A large man wreathed in a cloud of steam struggled to open the engine compartment. A smaller figure held a large plastic container. A spot of pink sat inside the car. And then they were gone.

'Dad, that's that car!' Samuel's voice was shrill.

'Sure was, Sam. And serves him right too!'

'Was anyone hurt?' Alex asked, genuinely concerned.

'No. They've just blown a water hose or a radiator. Maybe their pride is hurt,' Greg added. 'I hope so anyway. The silly idiots deserve a very long walk home.' He smiled at Fionna then called over his shoulder, 'Nearly there.'

Alex and Samuel let out an unrestrained 'Yaaaay!'

Before long, their station wagon slowed for the tight turn on to the access road, and shortly, Greg had unlocked the padlock and draped the chain over the post that proudly bore the sign 'Ōmahanui'. They bumped their way along the narrow driveway that meandered up and down through bush and overhanging tree ferns until a short burst of the engine brought them over the last rise. And there before them was the house.

'What the—' Greg began.

The station wagon stopped abruptly. The front door to the house was half open inwards, and shattered glass snarled at them through a jagged hole.

CHAPTER 2

Ōmahanui

'Stay here,' Greg said.

'Be careful, won't you?' Fionna said as he eased out of the driver's seat. Her face was tight and anxious.

Greg walked casually towards the open door without answering. He paused and inspected the broken glass, then looked more closely at the door frame. Using his handkerchief like a glove, he pushed the door so it opened inwards all the way. No eye blinked in the station wagon.

'Bring the camera, will you, Alex?' he called.

Fionna hurriedly unbuckled her seat belt. 'Stay there,' she said to Alex as she took the camera from the glove box.

Alex and Samuel watched as their parents talked earnestly together. Greg took pictures from several angles, and some close-ups, before handing back the camera. Fionna returned to the car.

'Dad says it's OK to get out.' Then as the two scrambled from their seats, she added, 'But watch out for glass.'

'Has anything been stolen, Dad?' Samuel craned his neck to see inside.

'Don't know yet, Sam. I'm going to treat it as a crime scene, so I don't want you touching anything, OK? That means you can't go inside unless I tell you.'

Greg returned to the car, and taking his cell phone from the car door pocket, he was soon talking in a business-like manner, pacing back and forth, explaining with his free arm to the person on the other end. Finally he closed the phone and came back towards them.

'We're not the only ones. They've had three other break-ins reported in the area, and there will probably be others as people arrive for their holidays. Russell police say they'll send someone as soon as they can, but it might not even be until tomorrow. I'll go inside and check what's been taken.'

Shortly he returned. 'All the food and drink has gone, but everything else seems fine. Even the television is still there.'

His face was a mixture of relief and questioning. 'It's probably kids,' he said, exploring a possibility. Pointing to marks on the aluminium door frame and the door jamb, he continued, 'They tried to force the door, then when that didn't work, they broke the glass and unlocked it from the inside.' Samuel looked intently at each thing his father pointed out.

Meanwhile, Alex was digesting both scene and information. Her brow wrinkled. Something didn't seem right. Her eyes moved from one thing to another as their voices faded behind her thoughts. And then it came to her.

'Dad,' she interrupted, 'if they smashed the glass to get in, why is the broken glass outside and almost none inside?' There was silence as everyone checked the detail.

'Well, well.' Greg spoke slowly with a strange smile on his face. 'You are absolutely right.' His lips pursed. 'Well, well,' he repeated. 'That changes things.' His voice became more animated. 'What's more, there's a deadlock on this door, so they couldn't reach in and open the door unless they had a key and . . .' His voice trailed off.

Understanding grew. Someone had a key and then had tried to make it look as though it was a break-in. Why?

'Well,' said Fionna in a voice designed to dispel alarm, 'we can't do anything more about this until the police arrive, so how about we get our gear down to the bach.'

The bach was about one hundred steep metres down through bush to the beach. In recent years, a cable trolley, running on angle iron rails, had been installed by a work party of grandparents, uncles, and cousins. Grandly called the train, it was designed with two seats in tandem to transport older adults, heavy bags and provisions, and the occasional child as a treat. When rain made the foot track dangerously slippery, rules on age might be relaxed.

Both Alex and Samuel worked energetically helping take loads from the station wagon to the small shelter to which someone had humorously attached a sign that said, 'Piccadilly Station'. This day was one time they were instructed to ride the train. Bags and cartons and loose bedding needed to be held securely by bodies that didn't take up too much space.

Alex sat in the front seat among the first load with her arms spread wide, hands tightly grasping anything likely to shift. Samuel sat behind her, almost hidden by his share of the load.

'OK, Samuel?'

''Course.'

Alex pressed the green button that kicked the electric winch into life. This was the most important time to hold on to things. For several seconds, the train was in free fall until the spring softened cable jerked taut and governed its speed to that of the cable drum.

Although the grinding clatter of the cable gears was loud at Piccadilly Station, it soon faded as the rails curved over the slope and the train slowly descended through the tunnel of trees. The gentle rumbling of rubber wheels and the intermittent scraping of cable on rusted rollers evoked memories of past holidays. Alex raised her face to the canopy, inhaled the sun-warmed scent of kānuka trees and smiled broadly. Her father scrambled alongside, occasionally falling behind, but as they neared the landing, he moved ahead.

The automatic cut-out brought the train to an easy halt beside the landing just above the bach. An outside toilet formed one wall of the landing, and the same humourist had attached the name 'Waterloo' to the safety rail. The delicious sound of small waves on the beach filled the silence. Greg expertly lifted off the baggage, and very quickly, the two were freed. Samuel immediately started for the beach.

'Where do you think you're going?' asked Greg, and when Samuel began a vague answer, he cut in, 'There's plenty of time for that.' He handed them some plastic bags that bulged with supermarket goods. 'Put these carefully on the bench by the door.'

Alex descended the small flight of wooden steps that led down to the covered deck.

'Hold on,' said Dad. 'We might as well take them straight inside. I'll come and unlock.'

Alex stopped at the doorway. The hair on the back of her neck stood stiff and tingling. 'Dad,' she wailed, 'the door's wide open!'

'It's just the same,' Greg reported to Fionna. 'All the food is gone. There might be a few other things we'll find missing when we go to use them, but even the outboard motor and the life jackets are still there. It'll be the same scumbags—that's for sure. They probably came in from the beach and did the bach over before following the train track to find the house up here.'

'I can telephone for someone to repair the doors. You and the children can go on taking the rest of the gear down to the bach if you like,' Fionna suggested.

'Not a bad idea. See if they can come tomorrow afternoon just in case the cops can't come until tomorrow morning. If they can get some fingerprints, it could be helpful.' It amused Alex to hear her father calling the police 'cops'.

There were five further trips on the train, and Samuel, desperate to get onto the beach, began whingeing about the unfairness of life. Although Fionna was sure to rearrange things the way she liked, the gear was finally stored, and Greg dismissed the two to the beach before returning in the empty train to fetch her.

The tide was almost full in, severely restricting their movement above the high-water mark. Samuel's frustration made him unbearable company, so Alex forced her way through the low-hanging kowhai tree branches in the opposite direction from her brother and waded along the water's edge towards the boat shed. Kawakawa and lemonwood saplings had quickly added their camouflage to the sprawling pōhutukawa boughs that masked the shed from passing boats and the occasional group that landed to picnic on the beach. Bush-green corrugated iron doors slept blindly before her. At least the boat shed was still secure.

And then she saw it. Recent rain had made the ground soggy. Among the leaf mould and clay, several foot impressions led along one side of the boat shed. Behind the shed, a barely discernible track began. Alex followed it to where the bush began to climb steeply. Now a series of slip marks defined the track. Tiny rivulets seeped from them. Someone had used the track very recently.

Samuel was eager to follow the track but Greg was very firm. 'It could be the same person who broke into our house and bach. It could give Russell police further clues, so let's leave it to them first. If they're not interested, then we can go up.'

He turned to Alex. 'Good spotting, girl. That's two things today. A proper young detective you are.'

He smiled a warm smile, and Alex responded modestly, 'Just a bit lucky, that's all.' Nevertheless, an enormous elation filled her chest, and she felt her face redden.

Her father led the way back. The tide had nearly reached the flax plants that marked high water, so they waded up to their knees in the clear water until they reached the gap in the flax that hid the short path leading up the side of the bach. Mum had some plates of sandwiches and a cane basket of fruit on the old Formica table.

'You must be half starved to death,' she said. 'Come and get it.'

For the next few minutes few words were spoken. Finally, Fionna said, 'Well? Is anyone going to tell me what you found?'

Samuel began to speak, but Greg cut him short. 'We have another detective in the family. Alex has definitely found something interesting, but if the boys consider it important, we'll let them deal with it.' He was referring to the local police. 'Oh, and that reminds me,' he continued, 'Someone should be up there in case they arrive this afternoon.'

He scraped his chair over the floorboards as he stood. 'I think Samuel should come with me. OK, boy?' Samuel was instantly on his feet, swallowing a large wad of half-chewed food. He grabbed another sandwich and headed for the door.

Greg winked at Alex and said, 'The girls might like some quiet time on their own. Alex, you can tell Mum what you discovered.'

Handing him some fruit in a plastic bag, Fionna asked, 'Is the intercom on?'

'I'll do it now,' he said, flicking a switch on the wall. Immediately a red light glowed on the small black communication unit that sat on the bench near the door. 'All done. I'll let Samuel call down when we arrive to check it's working properly.' And then they were gone. The intercom was a simple press-and-talk device that had been there ever since Alex could remember. When her grandparents stayed in the house while her family was in the bach, it certainly saved a lot of legwork up and down the hill, taking messages or getting information. Grandpa and Gran were unusually fit for people of their age, and they frequently walked the track rather than using the train. They said it was good for them, but if the track was slippery, the intercom was very useful for quick messages. Samuel especially liked to call to tell them how many fish he had caught and Grandpa would tease him about the number or size of the fish, and as Greg said, Samuel always 'rose to the bait'.

Alex told her mother what she had discovered as they ate fruit at the table. Fionna gave several concerned glances in the direction of the boat shed, hesitated and then said, 'I'm sure Dad will sort it all out. There is nothing for us to be worried about.' Alex sensed her mother was saying this as much for herself as for her.

Alex surveyed the bach. It was essentially one large room. A double divan bed filled the far corner, and beside it, reclaimed French doors led off to an outside deck. To the right of these doors was a small refrigerator. Above it and along the next wall, simple wooden shelves held an untidy collection of crockery. A window over the kitchen sink interrupted the shelves, letting in bush-filtered light. The kitchen bench that Alex vaguely remembered seeing in her grandparents' home ended at the damaged door. Curtains hung from the edge of the bench, concealing shelves of saucepans, roasting trays, food containers, and an ancient gas cylinder for the stove. Open shelves above the bench bore the collection of canned goods and packets of food they had brought down on the train. Alex caught sight of a purple packet: Whole Brazil Nuts. She smiled. 'Holy Breezles' was what her father had read when he was young. Now all the family called them that.

Beyond the door, four bunks—two above two—were fixed to the wall close to the train landing. A dividing curtain could be drawn at night to separate this sleeping area from the rest of the room. Windows occupied most of the seaward wall, and blue curtains matching the room divider could cover them at night. Two electric bulbs with collar shades hung from white ceiling tiles.

Most things in the bach were family items, initially too good to throw away and later with so much sentimental value that any suggestion they be disposed of met with fierce resistance. The old Formica table had been a wedding gift for Gran and Grandpa. The cluster of ancient cane chairs around the table was from Aden. Gran's father had stowed them on his naval ship when returning from Queen Elizabeth's coronation.

'Hello. Anyone there?' Samuel's reedy voice squeezed from the black box by the door.

Fionna quickly reached for the button. 'Hello, Samuel. I can hear you loud and clear. Over.'

'Hi, Mum. Mum, guess what. The boys arrived just as we got to the house. They've got four-wheel drives up here, not like the police cars back in Auckland. And they're dusting the door for fingerprints. Over.'

Everyone had adopted this communication jargon. It made good sense as only one voice could transmit at a time and it let you know when the other had finished.

'That's very good to hear, Sam. Are they going to come down here as well? Over.'

'Hold on. I'll ask them.' In his excitement, he forgot the end-of-send procedure.

'Yep.' The voice came back. 'And Dad says they want a cup of coffee. Can you put the water on? Over.'

'Do they indeed?' Fionna said before pressing the button again. 'OK. Tell Dad I'll have it ready. Over and out.'

'Good one, Mum. Over and out.'

Alex had already gone to the sink and was filling the kettle. Fionna let her place it on the stove and light the gas ring.

Before the kettle had boiled, the distant sound of the winch could be heard humming in the rails out from the bunk wall. When the squeaking wheels alerted them to their near arrival, Alex went out to meet the train.

The bulky forms of the two policemen dressed in police-supply summer shorts, their knees pulled up in front and boy-like smiles on their faces, was comical. The train stopped with a small jolt against the stopper. Greg and Samuel shuffled down the last few steps of the track and jumped on to the landing.

'Man, that's awesome,' said the younger of the two policemen as he clambered from the front seat. The train moved a little up the track with his weight removed.

'What was that you said when we were free-falling at the start?' teased his older and heavier colleague. 'You said—'

'Ladies present, boys,' Greg cut in quickly. Samuel's face showed that he had heard what was said. It had that 'I shouldn't actually repeat it but I'll give you a sort of idea' look on it.

'And I guess this is the smart young detective we've been hearing about,' said the younger of the two. 'Hi, I'm Jeff, and this old fella behind is Marcus.'

He extended his hand to her. Although taken by surprise and a little embarrassed, Alex sensed a genuine gesture. Both of their handshakes were firm. She led the way into the bach, the policemen briefly looking at the splintered wood around the door latch before entering and commenting about the view of the water through the facing windows.

The men looked oddly out of place in the bach. Maybe it was their size. They certainly took up a lot of room. Or could it have been the sight of their strong legs in boots, topped by short trousers.

Meanwhile, Fionna had been introduced, and friendly banter was taking place. Greg enjoyed this sort of light-hearted conversation, but

Fionna excused herself and, with Alex's help, poured the coffee and brought out the home baking stored in plastic containers under the kitchen bench. Samuel watched silently, glad to be part of the scene as his father and the policemen talked.

'Well, I guess we'd better look at your find, young lady.' Marcus rose from his chair. 'Thanks, Fionna. Great coffee,' he said. 'Now, which way?'

The tide had turned, but there was only a sliver of beach. Alex pointed out where they were headed, and while she, Greg, and Samuel waded, the two policemen, preferring to keep their boots on, forced a way through the undergrowth behind the flax.

At the boat shed, she pointed out what had first alerted her and then conducted them along the side of the shed to where the path climbed steeply upwards. They examined the slip marks closely.

'We'll go take a look. See what we can find,' said Marcus. 'No,' he responded to Samuel's eager request, 'you just stay here with your sister until we've checked everything, OK?'

Barely hiding his disappointment, Samuel went off to throw shells at the tide. Alex sat on a raised bank of shells, watching Samuel with mild amusement.

It was some time before they heard boots crunching on fallen ponga tree fronds, and heels digging heavily into the slippery track. There came a yelp from the bush above them followed by laughter and banter. Shortly they burst through the foliage and on to the beach.

Marcus's face was florid. A broad mud streak plastered his bare skin from ankle to thigh and continued up his trousers to his hip. Jeff was enjoying himself at his partner's expense.

'Like a drunk after closing time. You should have seen him. Got completely legless and kissed a tree on the way down.' He laughed loudly at his own description.

Marcus chose not to respond. He turned to Alex and, with mock severity asked, 'Have you been doing any gardening up there, young lady?'

Alex was confused. 'No. We only arrived today.' She felt her face redden. 'Is there a garden up there?'

'Well, there's certainly a lot of weed up there.'

'He means we have a little plantation,' Greg said. Alex didn't understand.

'A nice little cash crop,' Marcus added. 'I'd guess someone's been gardening maybe three to four months. Likely to be harvested pretty soon.'

Then turning to Greg, he continued, 'I'll speak to the sergeant when we get back to the truck. He can decide what we do about it.'

Despite the carefully guarded conversation, Alex suddenly caught on. 'Dad, is it cannabis?' she asked.

'Sure sounds like it.'

Alex looked at Samuel with glistening eyes. Adventure and mystery were what you read about, not what happens to you.

'It's drugs, Samuel. Marijuana. You know, dope,' Alex explained to her brother. 'Someone is growing it up there in the bush.'

'Wow,' said Samuel. 'Can we have a look, Dad?'

Dad looked at the two policemen. 'What do you reckon?'

'I guess we've already left enough tracks for the grower to know he's been sprung.' Jeff looked at Marcus, who nodded. 'Yeah. We've checked for booby traps, so it should be safe enough. Just take the usual precautions, and if you find anything helpful, either photograph it or write the normal report.'

The party retraced their steps to the bach, and after a friendly farewell to Fionna, Jeff and Marcus climbed into the tandem seats, Jeff taking the topmost seat this time. Greg pressed the button for them. Almost silently they began the ascent through the tree tunnel, and Greg followed, tackling the uphill track once more. Boy-like smiles lit the policemen's faces again, and they waved down at Samuel until swallowed by the bush.

It was approaching six o'clock, and the late afternoon sun reflected brightly off the sea into the bach. Brother and sister sat on the window seat, their backs to the dazzle, separately occupying themselves. It was difficult to settle to anything, their concentration captive to the day's events. Mum busied herself preparing the evening meal.

'I'll do those if you like, Mum,' Alex offered and, taking the peeler from her, began to scrape at the potatoes, relieved to have a purposeful task to occupy her mind.

'There's some carrots too, if you feel like it.' Her mother appreciated some help, but sometimes she loaded the task up a bit. Today, Alex didn't mind at all.

'When is Dad coming back?' Samuel asked, impatience barely contained. 'It'll be too dark by the time he gets back. We'll never get to see the mariwara.'

'Marijuana,' Alex corrected.

'Well we won't get to see that either,' Samuel complained. 'Why is everything so frustrating?'

He threw the Lego car he had been making towards his bed. It hit the edge of the bed and dropped to the floor in several bits. This proved too much to cope with. He launched from his seat and tore the remaining pieces apart and began throwing them at the wall.

'Samuel, go and see how much beach there is. If there's enough, I'll get you to light a small fire later, so we can toast marshmallows for dessert. Go on,' Fionna instructed, as her plan to prise him from his ill humour seemed to falter. 'There's a good boy.'

He was smart enough to know he was being manipulated, but not old enough to resist the temptation. Reluctantly, he edged off his bed 'I bet it'll still be too high,' he said.

Gloom followed him out the door. Shortly he returned, his humour already improved. 'No, it's good,' he reported. 'Can I get some wood ready, Mum?'

'Yes, but remember you won't be lighting it just yet.' He scuttled off in search of brush and driftwood.

'He's young yet.' Fionna sensed Alex's annoyance.

'Was I ever like him?' she asked.

'Yes, quite a bit,' Fionna replied. 'Not the same,' her mother assured her. 'You used to put on the sulks rather than get angry like Samuel.' She looked across at her daughter. 'But you're over that now. You're not a little girl anymore.' She was about to say something more but thought better of it. A thud on the landing announced Greg's return. Alex raced out to greet him.

'Are we allowed to go up the track, Dad? Did the sergeant say it was all right? Can we see the marijuana?'

'Whoa. Back down, girl. Yes, we're allowed to. But I'm pretty knackered. I've been up and down the track nine times today.' Then noting the disappointment on her face, he added, 'OK, shoes on. If we get going immediately, we'll probably make it. The light is going pretty fast. I don't want us to be coming back down in the dark. Where's Samuel?'

Collecting Samuel from the beach, Alex gave him the shoes she had selected, and they caught up with their father, who had continued walking along the recently exposed sand.

After the glare off the water, the bush seemed dark, but their eyes gradually adjusted as they eagerly climbed the steep track by grasping at trunks of trees and occasional saplings. Two summers ago, Alex with some cousins had even braved scary 'possums and slept in tents on the ridge overnight.

As they neared the ridge, Greg paused. The track had petered out. He scouted around, and then without warning, a large cluster of dark green plants filled a clearing before them. An expanse of camouflage netting some three metres above them was secured by ropes tied to a number of trees. In this way, the plot was hidden from helicopters or light planes. He began to point out how marijuana plants could be recognised by their thin serrated leaves arranged in a distinct pattern and growing, at this stage, on strong stalks up to two metres high.

'What's wrong with marijuana?' Alex's question puzzled her father.

'Haven't you been told about it at school?' he asked.

'Well, they just said it's against the law and it's a drug that some people get addicted to and we need to be older before we decide whether to try it or not.'

'Did they really?' He gave a sigh. 'Let me tell you both, it causes a lot of crime and a lot of people wreck their lives with it. We see it all the time. So now you've seen what it looks like, you'll be able to tell the police if you come across it again. But you've got to be extremely careful, because there are some very nasty people involved. Whoever is growing this is either not very skilled or they didn't think it would be discovered, because there are no booby traps to protect it from being stolen. If you ever find any, don't go near. You could end up being shot or speared or some other things you don't want to hear about.'

'I do, Dad. What sort of things?' Samuel asked.

Greg ignored him and moved off. 'Come on, then—it'll be darker once we leave the ridge. The cicadas will stop singing any time now, then you'll know it's too late.' For the first time since their arrival, Alex became aware of cicadas filling the sky with their summer orchestration, their sound so much part of summer that it barely reached her conscious mind.

Chapter 3

Russell

Blast!' Greg exclaimed as the Russell petrol station came into view. 'I forgot to bring the fuel tanks. We'll have to use the dinghy until I come back again. It's fishing from off the beach meanwhile, Samuel. Sorry.'

'That's all right, Dad. I can get some good ones off the rocks as well.' Samuel was in good spirits.

Fionna clasped a long list of items to replace the stolen food. Greg planned to meet the handyman at the hardware store to decide on the door handle and replacement lock.

With New Year's Eve just four days away, the town was bustling, and parking was hard to find. Eventually they found a spot in a back street alongside the primary school field.

'You two stick together,' Fionna instructed as they slammed their doors behind them.

'I need you both back at the car by 12.30. Don't make me have to come looking for you,' Greg called after them.

was Samuel who made the discovery. 'Hey! It's that old bomb.'

They were passing the petrol station, and in the service bay, Alex recognised the battered vehicle. In the dimness, she made out the raised bonnet and guessed the repair was to fix the massive steam blow-out they had glimpsed. She hoped the driver wasn't around and, if he was, that he wouldn't recognise them.

Samuel had moved on quickly to look in the small window of the fishing tackle and repairs shop. Alex joined him and, for a short while, pretended to be interested in the objects he pointed out before suggesting they get an ice cream. Samuel led the way along the waterfront to the ice-cream parlour. They sat on one of the weathered wooden benches facing the sea, contentedly licking their ice creams.

The outline of Paihia stretched along the opposite shoreline either side of two small islands, its hills randomly studded with houses pressed into the dark green bush. A paraglider soared skywards behind a distant speck on the water. They both watched with interest until Samuel said, 'I'm going out on the wharf. Want to come?'

Alex thought briefly, then said, 'No. You go.' She rolled the legs of her board shorts up as far as they would comfortably go. 'I'll just get some suntan on my legs. Make sure you come back here. We're meant to stick together.' She watched him make his way to the wharf and begin threading through a jostle of new arrivals streaming off a ferry.

Her ice cream now finished, she kicked off her Jandals and crunched barefooted down the slope of fine red pebbles to the water's edge, enjoying the cool water lapping her ankles as she washed her hands.

By the time she returned to the seat, her hands were dry. She adjusted her shorts for the sun again, leaned back, and closed her eyes. The warmth was intoxicating. The babble of voices, putter of outboard motors, and murmur of cars receded, and she felt herself drifting.

'Gidday.'

The voice entered slightly into her consciousness.

'Gidday!' The voice came a little louder.

Alex opened her eyes, and a face came into focus. Instantly she was alert. A boy was looking down at her, his handsome brown face topped by a fringe of wavy black hair under a baseball cap worn peak backward. Laughter and mischief chased each other in the dark centres of his eyes. She immediately recognised the broad smile.

'You're . . . that boy.' She choked. Then as she gained composure, she added, 'You were in that car. You poked your tongue out at me.'

'Only because you were staring at me.'

'I was not! *You* were staring at me.'

'Why would I stare at *you*? There's nothing much to look at.'

Alex felt a desperate urge to roll down the legs of her shorts.

He continued, 'But I can see why you would stare at *me*, 'cause I'm so good-looking, eh. Nah, you were definitely looking at me.' He lifted his cap and ran a hand through his sleek hair.

'You gave me a fright.'

'You're pretty easy to scare.' After a short pause, he asked, 'What's your name?'

Alex hesitated. He was arrogant and boastful. He had no right to know her name. For a moment she thought of giving a stupidly false name, like Gertrude or Esmeralda, or to tell him to mind his own business. But then she reasoned she would actually like to know his name, and that would probably ruin her chances.

'It's Alex.'

He looked at her inquiringly, a small wrinkle forming above his nose. 'That's a boy's name. You're kidding me, right?'

'No. That's my name. Well, it's Alexandra really, but everyone calls me Alex. Well, nearly everyone.' Her grandpa always called her Alexandra.

'Alexandra. That's a real cool name.'

Alex noted that the laughter and mischief had vanished from his eyes.

'Why do you let people call you Alex when Alexandra sounds just like you look?'

Alex decided to ignore the question. 'Well, I told you my name. What's yours?'

'Hāmuera.' Then seeing the lack of recognition, he said, 'It's a Māori name. I'm a Māori.'

Alex had guessed that much. 'Do you live up here?' she asked more out of politeness than interest.

'Nah, I just come up for holidays. Once I came up for a month when my mum went to hospital. I had to go to the school behind the shops over there.' He indicated with his head. 'Some of my whānau live up here. I live in Ōtāhuhu.' He spoke with true Māori pronunciation.

Alex knew roughly where that was—an old suburb in South Auckland.

'So where do *you* live?'

'On the North Shore. Northcote.'

Hāmuera looked blank.

'Never been there. Is it nice?'

'Really nice.'

They both fell silent. Alex really wanted to roll the legs of her board shorts down, but the boy was still standing in front of her, shifting his weight from one leg to the other and looking away to the wharf from time to time. Neither knew how to end the silence. Alex guessed he would like to sit down. If he did, she felt she would have to make an excuse to get up and leave. It was becoming embarrassing.

Relief came in the form of Samuel. 'Alex, there's heaps of sprats around the end of the wharf and they're catching lots.' Suddenly he noticed the boy. 'Hello,' he said.

'Gidday. You're the little brother.'

'How do you know me?' Samuel frowned, trying to dredge up a memory of him.

Alex found her voice. 'He's the boy in that car yesterday.'

Recognition dawned. 'Your car nearly ran up our exhaust. Your driver was crazy.' The words came out before he thought, then realising he might have said something offensive, Samuel back-tracked. 'I mean, he drives like a maniac.' Somehow the correction didn't sound any better and he stopped in pink-cheeked confusion.

'That's my cousin all right. He doesn't do slow. He nearly broke the car yesterday. I thought it was on fire, but it was just steam.' A throaty chuckle escaped his mouth. 'We towed it to the garage this morning, and they say they can put a second-hand radiator in it. Probably cost a bomb though.'

It is a bomb. The thought was better inside her head than spoken. Instead Alex said, 'Samuel saw it in the garage as we went past.'

'Hey, you and me've got the same name.' He grinned at Samuel.

'No you haven't,' Alex objected. 'You've got a Māori name. You told me.'

'Samuel in Māori is Hāmuera,' he said matter-of-factly. 'My teachers call me Sam.' He turned back to Samuel, and another chuckle erupted. 'It's better than Ham, eh?' He looked at Samuel, and the two boys laughed.

'If they called you Ham, that would mean you were a little pig.'

Hāmuera's eyes widened and then eased into smile lines. 'You're a cheeky little fella, aren't you? If you don't get too smart, we could be mates. Do you like fishing?' Then hearing Samuel's eager response, he said, 'Well, I know where the best fishing in all of the Bay of Islands is. Maybe I could show you some time. Where do you stay up here?'

Alex sensed he was asking for reasons other than taking Samuel fishing.

'Where is our place, Alex?' Samuel asked.

'Ōmahanui,' Alex said, quickly supplying the name her great grandparents had given the property many years before. It worked. Hāmuera showed no sign of recognition. 'Never heard of it,' he said, 'but it must be pretty awesome 'cause in Māori it means "place of great pleasure". Where exactly is it?'

'Near Jack's Bay.' Samuel was pleased to help.

Now the locality was revealed, Alex added against her better judgement, 'Clendon Point.' She noticed an instant change in the Māori boy's face. 'Do you know it?' she asked.

'I don't think so,' he answered vaguely, but Alex sensed he knew more than he was admitting.

Then taking the initiative, she asked, 'And what about you? Where are you staying?'

'Why do *you* want to know? Oh, I know. You want to come and visit me, eh, 'cause I'm so good-looking.' He removed his cap and flicked at his hair again, striking a pose.

'In your dreams,' she retorted, but the roguish grin on his face quickly melted her annoyance. He was teasing again. 'You haven't told me yet. Where do you stay?' she insisted.

'My aunty's place—Ōponga.' He forced his face into mock seriousness and, with dramatic expression, said, 'But you got to promise not to visit me there. My aunty doesn't like me going out with pākehā girls. She says I got to marry a Māori girl.'

Although she knew he was still teasing her, the grin that followed was less convincing than before.

'Is he your boyfriend, Alex?' Samuel looked excited.

'He certainly is not,' said Alex with feeling. 'I only met him this morning, and he's far too arrogant for my liking.'

'And she's a bit ugly for me. My girlfriends are all models, beautiful like me.' He paused for a moment. 'Nah, we could be friends, but not girlfriend and boyfriend, eh.'

Alex bit her lower lip and decided the conversation was over. 'We've got to go now,' she said airily, and indicated to Samuel to follow her. 'Our dad wants us back at the car by twelve o'clock.'

'No. Dad said half past twelve,' Samuel argued.

Alex gave him an exasperated look. 'Don't argue,' she hissed at him. 'Come on.'

'I'll see you around some time,' Hāmuera called at their retreating backs. 'Maybe at your place . . . Alexandra.'

Alex was definitely annoyed now. She knew he was still teasing, trying to get her to bite back, and she wasn't going to give him that satisfaction. Instead she took it out on her young brother so that by the time she arrived at their station wagon, he had dropped well behind and was feeling very sorry for himself.

An informal game of football was under way on the school field. Alex sat in the shade of the boundary trees, glad she was not one of the players with the sun beating down upon her, and watched their movements without any real interest. Samuel flopped onto the grass a small distance away. His expression made her feel bad. After a while, she said, 'I'm sorry, Samuel.'

He didn't answer.

'I had to make an excuse to get away from that boy. I'm sorry. I shouldn't have got snarky with you.'

'I told the truth and you yelled at me.' His voice quavered with emotion and his voice got louder. 'It's not fair! I told the truth and you yelled at me. Anyway, he's my friend and he's going to show me where to fish . . . and you can't come.'

The last three words were said with finality and seemed to make him feel better. Shortly he asked, 'What was his name again?'

Alex felt like saying, *If he's your friend, you should know his name,* but in the interest of healing wounded feelings she answered, 'Hāmuera.'

Samuel repeated the name several times then, satisfied he would remember it, began watching the soccer game. It was very one-sided, and after a while, the losing players lost interest and drifted off to the sidelines.

'*There* you are.' Greg's voice startled them both. 'Would someone like to go and help Mum?' He indicated down the road with a jerk of his head as he placed a number of bulging supermarket bags into their station wagon.

Fionna was very grateful for the assistance. Samuel arrived first and took the largest bag. Alex took a smaller bag, leaving her mother to carry a heavier one in each hand at her insistence.

'Whew, it's hot,' said Fionna as she deposited the bags in the wagon and rubbed the circulation back into numbed fingers. 'Let's get in and get the air conditioning on.'

'Anyone hungry yet?' Greg asked as he pulled on to the road. The smell of freshly baked bread filled the car. There was plenty of choice now the shopping had been done, and suggestions became more and more fanciful as the back-seat passengers competed for the most outrageous combinations. Eventually, pickled onion and prune sandwiches with mustard sauce won. Their laughter became more hysterical when Fionna threatened to make one for them.

They were descending through the tight corners to the quarry when Greg said, 'I don't believe it. Look what's up ahead.'

They were fast catching up to a familiar car trailing a thin haze of smoke, driving slowly along the flat stretch beside Frenchman's Swamp.

'I'm going to pass him before the twisty bits,' said Greg. 'Otherwise we won't get home before dinner time.'

He accelerated and the gap closed quickly, but not quickly enough to pass before the right-hand bend loomed. He braked and settled in behind until he could see clear road ahead. Just as he indicated and pulled out to pass, the car in front spurted a cloud of smoke and accelerated also. Another bend appeared before he could safely pass. He braked and slid in behind again.

'He did that deliberately,' Greg fumed.

Fionna gave him a concerned look. 'It doesn't matter about taking longer. Let him go.'

Greg eased off the accelerator and the car in front slowed also, until both vehicles had reduced to walking pace.

'This is ridiculous!' Greg spat. A quick glance in the rear-view mirror, a savage thrust on the indicator stalk and he pulled out to pass, but again the offender sped up, causing Greg to brake for the rapidly closing blind bend. The passenger turned and looked back through the rear window. A Māori boy's face grinned at them.

'That's Hāmuera,' Samuel exclaimed, waving at him through the gap between his parents. 'He's my friend.' A friendly wave came back.

'What do you mean he's your friend? How do you know his name?' asked Greg, his eyes fixing briefly on Samuel from the rear-view mirror.

'We met him down by the wharf,' Alex answered quickly, hoping to stop any embarrassing comment from her young brother. That was wishful thinking.

'Yeah, and he wants to be her boyfriend.'

'He does not!' Alex said indignantly.

'Don't talk silly, Samuel,' Fionna warned. 'That only causes arguments.'

Greg was determined to pass. 'I've had enough of this.'

A short straight stretch of road came into view, and he thrust his right foot to the floor. The offending vehicle burped smoke and sped up but couldn't match the Subaru's power this time. There was just enough road to swerve back to the left before the fast-approaching corner. Tyres protested loudly in the bend, and the back-seat passengers were thrown to one side.

'Greg, that's enough,' Fionna growled. 'That's dangerous.'

He let the car slow a little but, with frequent glances in the rear-view mirror, kept driving faster than normal. Samuel in particular enjoyed the cornering and exaggerated the way he rolled towards Alex. As Samuel was in a good mood again, Alex chose to ignore it.

By the time the signpost to Jack's Bay appeared, the road behind was empty, and shortly, the leafy shade of the driveway leading to the house enclosed them. Cicada rasping filled the summer silence the moment the motor stopped. Scorching heat grabbed at their skin as they left the air-conditioned sanctuary of the car.

'A pity the tide is low,' Fionna said. 'We could do with a swim, I reckon. It might cool us all down.' The subtle message was lost on Greg.

'All in good time. Everyone take something down to the train.' Greg organised the supermarket bags into willing hands. 'Let Mum and Alex go down with all this stuff,' he instructed Samuel. 'You and I can walk down.'

They watched the train begin its descent with both passengers holding firmly to the morning's purchases before taking to the track.

'Samuel, the fewer people who know this place is here, the better. Local Māori have a bad reputation, so I'm not keen on you making friends with them, is that understood?' He spoke evenly and with intent. 'It's probably them who broke into our place.'

'Hāmuera wouldn't do that,' Samuel protested.

'Maybe not, but he's a cheeky young brat anyway and I don't want you mixing with him, OK?'

Samuel was disappointed. 'But, Dad, he likes fishing and he's going to show me the best places to fish around here.'

Greg cut him short. 'No, Samuel. And I hope you haven't invited him around. You haven't, have you?'

'No,' Samuel replied defensively.

'Good. I'll let your sister know too.'

Samuel concentrated on his footing. He had learned that when Dad gave an instruction, argument was useless.

A battered brown car was grinding up the steep rise from Dick's Bay. Inside, a large tattooed man was talking to his passenger.

'They think they can come up here in their flash cars and turn up their noses at us like we are muck from the cow shed. That's why I give them a hard time on the road, eh.' He snorted before continuing, 'So who owned all this land and the sea before the pākehā came, eh?'

The passenger quickly replied, 'Our tribe, Ngāpuhi.'

'And who was it warned us that the pākehā was not to be trusted, that pākehā would take our land and our fish from us?'

'Hone Heke.'

'And was he right?'

The boy hesitated. 'We sold a lot of it, didn't we? The land, I mean.'

The man stared intently at his passenger for a moment, and then keeping one eye on the road, he thrust a thick finger in his direction. 'You just remember this and don't forget it. Ngāpuhi are the rightful owners of everything here, the land and the sea too. Pākehā took it off us. That's why we are poor and they're rich. How much land is ours now, eh? Why can't we take kai moana from the sea without getting the pākehā's licence, eh?'

Hāmuera nodded. It was better not to argue with cousin Piri when he talked on this subject. Several court appearances and fines for exceeding fishing limits and taking shellfish out of season had soured him even more.

Piri swore loudly and spat out the window as he turned off the road. The car bumped through a narrow gap between mānuka trees. 'We Māori are getting busted because the pākehā changed the rules to suit themselves, eh. Don't you go mixing with those pākehā kids. You got that? Not even the kids can be trusted!'

Chapter 4

Discovery

'It's gone.' Greg's breath came quickly.

'What has?' Fionna looked up vaguely from her crossword.

'The cannabis—it's all gone. Not a bit left standing.'

Fionna's face immediately changed. 'But how could it? I mean, when could it?'

'I know, Dad,' Samuel offered. 'Jeff and Marcus came and took it while we were out.'

Greg's face looked thoughtful. He considered whether the police might have done so without calling first. 'That's a thought, but I'm pretty sure they would have let me know. I'd better go up to the house and give them a call. My mobile has no reception down here.'

'Can we go and have a look, Dad?' Samuel's eyes lit with excitement.

Greg hesitated. His first instinct was to say no, but in fact, there was no real reason why they shouldn't. The marijuana was gone. No obvious danger existed.

'As long as you take your mother with you, that should be OK. What do you say, Mum?' Fionna was taken by surprise. She hadn't yet ventured up the track to the plot and was hardly prepared for this.

'Do you think it really is a good idea, Greg? I mean, won't there be some clues or something, like Jeff and Marcus might . . . well, they could, couldn't they?' she stammered.

Samuel's eager face pleaded silently before her.

'Well, if you think it's all right.' She still looked a little doubtful.

'Come on, let's go,' said Samuel, heading for the door. 'Are you coming, Alex?'

Alex hesitated. Something uncomfortable lay in her mind like decayed leaves at the bottom of a bush pool: murky, vague, and not particularly pleasant. 'No, I'll just hang around here, I think. You go. I'll look after things, Mum.' She moved over to the bench where her mother had been preparing vegetables for dinner, surveying what yet needed to be done.

'Good girl,' Greg said, 'OK, I'll go up to the house and check with the boys.'

Fionna fussed around briefly, giving a few instructions to Alex before pulling on her trainers and following Samuel, who pranced excitedly down to the beach. Alex busied herself with the few instructions she had been given. The relative silence allowed her to think, the sort of thinking that switches instantly between reality and imagination.

Her tasks completed, Alex returned to her book, but by the time she had reached the bottom of the page, she no longer remembered what she had read. She started again, but as the bottom of the page loomed, her thoughts were distant from the words. A further attempt proved just as futile, so she dog-eared the page, tossed the book on to the tin trunk beside her bunk, and wandered the short distance down to the beach.

Though the sun was well on its way towards the hills, there was still plenty of heat and the sand beneath her bare feet was barely tolerable. The dinghy offered a cool seat in the shade of the kowhai tree, so seating herself on its stern, she gazed with unfocussed eyes through the low-hanging branches to the glittering water beyond.

Late afternoon sea breezes chased and teased the outgoing tide and the sun ricocheted off its ruffled surface. Even filtered through leaves, these reflections hurt her eyes, and she eased herself around with her back to the sea and her feet resting inside the boat.

It was as her eyes adjusted to the shadows that she noticed something on the bottom of the boat, beside her foot. A vaguely familiar but not immediately recognisable shape. For a brief moment, there was no connection. Then instantly, she became alert. It looked like . . . The moment she picked it up, she knew she was right. The leaf was long, slender, and saw-toothed along its edges. What was a marijuana leaf doing in their dinghy? A quick inspection found another two leaves.

Immediately she sprang from the dinghy and, pushing through the low-hanging branches, inspected the beach immediately before her. Now that she knew what to look for, it was very plain. For a distance of about five metres, there remained the groove of the dinghy's keel and several foot impressions in the sand and pebbles. Earlier in the day while they were away, the tide had been higher up the beach, and someone had dragged the dinghy from the water's edge to its position under the tree.

On an impulse, she pushed back under the branches and checked the securing rope at the bow. Everyone in the family had been taught to secure it around the trunk, but now it was tied loosely to a branch. Someone had used their dinghy to transport the marijuana while they were in Russell, and whoever it was had tried to conceal the fact.

The whirlpool of vague thoughts rotating in her head slowly formed a flowing line. Someone had stolen food items from the house and then broken the glass in the front door to make it look like it was a forced entry. But it couldn't have been because of where the broken glass lay outside. A key had to be used in the deadlock to open the door. Someone had a key to the house. Then the bach door had been forced. Once again, only food was taken. Someone had been growing marijuana on the property, and now it was gone. And someone had used the dinghy to take the plant material somewhere.

Alex frowned and her eyes narrowed. Someone had a key to the house, knew the marijuana had been discovered, knew when the family had first arrived and when they were out this morning. It was as if someone was close enough to spy on them. It was an unnerving thought.

A sudden inspiration came to her. 'That's it,' she whispered. 'That's it!' she repeated aloud. 'It has to be.'

She made her way the short distance back to the bach for some footwear and then at a fast jog to the boat shed. Once behind it, she began the steep scramble up the bush track. Almost immediately, she met Samuel awkwardly manoeuvring from tree trunk to tree trunk on a steep downward section. His face was all concentration and red from exertion. He paused with both arms wrapped around a kānuka tree trunk.

'You should have come up with us. Mum's just up there,' he puffed. 'And it *has* all gone, Alex. There's just stalks in the ground, and that net thing's gone. They just cut the ropes. They must have been in a hurry, Mum says.'

'I've got an idea, Samuel,' she interrupted. 'You might have to help me though. Will you come back up with me?'

His face contorted. 'Go back up there? I'm knackered.'

'Please, Samuel,' she pleaded. 'I think I might have solved some of the mystery, but I need someone who has good eyes to help me.' Samuel was slightly swayed. 'And someone who is not scared,' she added, appealing to his greatest vanity. He wavered. Alex waited. 'Dad thinks *I'm* a good detective. If you help me solve this, Dad will think *you* are too.' She held her breath. To be better than his sister was her brother's other vanity.

'I *am* a good detective. I was the one who noticed they had cut the ropes to that net thing.' He paused. 'All right then, I'll come, but just so you don't get scared, OK?'

She couldn't deny she would feel spooked on her own when the wind lurked among the treetops and boughs creaked against each other, so Alex chose to ignore the accusation.

'Oh, you've decided to come after all.' Fionna was further up the track, using the same method of descent as Samuel. She peered between two tree trunks. 'You should have come with us, Alex. I don't really want you going up there on your own now.'

'Samuel's going to come up with me, Mum. We'll be right.'

'Alex and I are going to solve the mystery, aren't we, Alex?' Samuel chimed in.

'We'll be right,' repeated Alex. 'We'll look after each other, and we won't stay there too long. Come on, Mum. We'll be just fine.'

'I guess so.' Fionna made her way carefully down to where the two had stood to the side of the track to let her through. 'But if Dad or I call, you must call back straight away, OK?'

'Trust us, Mum.'

Mum smiled. 'I do,' she replied. Then as the two set off, she called after them, 'Just don't give me cause to worry about you.'

In no time, the children were hidden by ponga fronds and tree trunks. Fionna found herself sliding and running down the final slope, grateful for the corrugated iron wall of the boat shed to halt her headlong rush.

'Just look for any sign of a shelter,' Alex instructed her brother. 'It might be a bivouac of ponga and bark, a tarpaulin, or tent fly over a frame, possibly even a whole tent, I just don't know. I think it will be hidden, probably not on the top of the ridge here. Almost for sure it will be on quite flat ground but not too far away from here. You got all that?'

Samuel nodded. She indicated towards the end of Clendon Point. 'OK, you go along that way, and I'll go this way,' she said. 'Call out if you find anything. And don't get scared all on your own in the bush,' she added smugly.

To the east, the ridge fell steeply into Jack's Bay. Not much chance of flat ground there. Nevertheless, Alex methodically checked it. The view across to Dick's Bay was mostly uninterrupted by trees, and behind the bay, bush-covered hills reclined in mellow late afternoon tones. A clear sky and dying breeze promised another calm, moonlit evening.

Bush grew luxuriant and tall down the side they had just climbed, and Alex explored a number of likely sites without success. Her eyes searched keenly for any sign that might lead to a shelter: foot marks, broken twigs, flattened grass, or a casually discarded item. Either she had missed something or there was nothing to find. Nagging disappointment prodded as she retraced her steps.

Samuel was waiting for her. 'Nothing,' he said, confirming her observation.

'Me neither.' Alex flopped down in front of him and explained. 'What I thought was, whoever broke into our house and bach was looking for food because they were sort of camping near this marijuana to guard it in case someone else found where it was and tried to steal it. I think it's worth a lot of money, 'cause it's drugs. And there's another thing, Samuel, but it's a bit scary.'

Samuel straightened up.

'I think someone knew when we arrived and has been watching us.'

'True?' he asked. His eyes showed concern. 'How do you know?'

'Well, think about it. Someone must have known the marijuana had been discovered and they knew we were away this morning, so it was their chance to cut it and take it away.' She hesitated before continuing in a dramatic way. 'I know how they took it away too.'

'How?'

'I found some marijuana leaves in our dinghy before I came up here, and foot marks in the sand. They used our boat to take the stuff away.' Samuel was all ears as she continued. 'The dinghy was tied up to a branch, not around the trunk like we always do it. Whoever it was didn't want us to know what they had done, Samuel, but he made a couple of mistakes, and we're on to him now. So where the heck has this person been hiding?'

'Could be persons, like more than one,' Samuel suggested.

'Well, however many of them there are, they must have had a good idea of what we were doing and how long we would be away.'

Alex rolled over on to her back and reviewed everything carefully. Clumps of kānuka branches etched the pale sky above her, occasionally stirred by a passing breeze. Her eyes aimlessly followed the gentle movements.

A tui began its distinctive bell-like notes and whistles somewhere in the canopy. Alex searched the branches, hoping to see its cluster of white throat feathers. Before she could locate it, the beating of wings announced the arrival of another tui settling in a tree to her left. Soon the two birds engaged in a duel of sound, first one, then the other, then without regard for each other.

Suddenly, Alex stiffened. She sat up, peering intently.

'What is it, Alex?' her brother whispered, slightly alarmed. 'Is someone coming?'

Alex didn't answer as she got to her feet and began to walk without moving her eyes from one of the trees. Samuel followed her.

'What is it, Alex?' he repeated hoarsely.

'Got it!' The words exploded from her mouth. 'Samuel, I've found the hideout. Look up there.' She pointed up into the smoothly gnarled branches of an old pūriri tree where thick mounds of straplike leaves clustered. A cunningly constructed shelter could just be made out.

'Oh, wow!' Samuel exclaimed. 'A tree hut.'

They had been searching the ground and hadn't considered this possibility. An elevated position made absolute sense. Few would think to look upwards into a tree as they climbed the steep track, and from that position, a hidden watcher could assess the situation when intruders approached.

The two scrambled and slid through the undergrowth until they reached the base of the pūriri. Here was further proof. Small cleats nailed to one of the sloping boughs gave handholds and footholds. For a moment, panic battled reason. The possibility that the someone might still be in the tree hut gripped her stomach like a vice.

'Can I go up first, Alex?' Samuel had one foot on a cleat in readiness.

'Yes,' she replied, and straight away, felt a stab of guilt as her brother began to climb. She was endangering her brother because of her own fear. 'No, stop, Samuel! I should go first.'

Samuel, suddenly deaf, continued to climb.

'Samuel!' she called urgently. 'Stop now. I mean it!' But Samuel had reached the floor of the shelter, and gripping it with both hands, he was lifting one foot over the edge. The next moment, he had disappeared over the top. Alex stared briefly at the dark shape that had swallowed him before rapidly beginning her own climb. She was over halfway up when Samuel's head reappeared.

'Come and have a look, Alex. It's really great.'

As the edge of the floor came level with her head, she paused, gasping for breath. Her panic and swift climb had caught up with her.

'Don't pretend you can't hear me, Samuel,' she said sharply. 'What if someone was actually up here still? What do you think would have happened then?'

'There's no one here. Why would they still be here if there's nothing to watch out for?'

His logic was compelling, and Alex felt a little foolish for needlessly worrying. She pulled herself over the edge and on to the platform and surveyed the scene. The flooring was rough, but the construction felt firm. A low frame of teatree formed rafters over which a green tarpaulin had been draped then secured at floor level. Ponga and nikau fronds overlaid the tarpaulin, further camouflaging the roof and sides. Occupying almost half of the floor lay a crumpled sleeping bag, while an untidy mix of bottles and cans surrounded a simple gas burner in the remaining space. Balanced on top of the burner sat a cheap aluminium saucepan, blackened on the outside and food encrusted on the inside. A bloated plastic rubbish bag leant against the tarpaulin wall.

'It's not that great,' Alex said a little churlishly. 'There's hardly any room to do anything.'

Samuel was undeterred and rattled on about how he would have organised things if he had to keep watch there. To him, it was an adventure.

'Shhhh, Samuel! Listen!'

Samuel stopped in mid-sentence, mild alarm on his face. 'What?' he asked.

In the following silence, they both heard their father's voice calling from the beach below.

'Coming, Dad!' Alex shouted in her loudest voice, before turning to her brother and instructing him to take care on the downward climb. Once on the ground, they made their way down the newly familiar track as quickly as they could. Her father was surely going to be astounded at what she had found.

Chapter 5

Rubbish

A damp coolness surrounded the bach as Alex pulled on her jeans and sweater just before the train bumped on the stopper outside.

Jeff and Marcus were men on a mission this time. Their sergeant certainly wasn't happy. That the marijuana had been harvested before they had made a full investigation and destroyed it was not merely unfortunate, he had said; it was sloppy policing. The tree hut and observation of the family's movements was a sinister addition. To be so close but remain hidden meant this person knew his way around, and presumably, this same person had broken into both the bach and the house for supplies.

Marcus half grinned at Alex. 'Right now, I think our sarge would fire me and hire you if you were old enough. Smart work, young lady.'

This time, colour did not rush to her cheeks. 'Do you want me to show it to you, the hut, I mean?'

'Seeing how we couldn't find it ourselves, I guess you had better show us.'

'Otherwise we could spend all morning looking for it,' Jeff chipped in.

They followed Alex down the rough path beside the bach and, pushing through the dewy flax leaves, stepped on to the narrow strip of sand above the receding tide.

'You won't be able to see where they dragged the dinghy back,' Alex said. The policemen looked blank. 'Well, the tide has come in since,' she continued. They now looked confused.

'Oh, sorry. I didn't tell you about that,' Greg explained. 'You tell them, Alex.'

As she was relating her discovery of marijuana leaves in the dinghy, the marks on the sand, and the way the dinghy had been tied up, both men pushed under the overhanging kowhai branches to inspect the boat. The leaves were where she had left them, and Marcus carefully placed them in a sealable plastic bag. Jeff opened his notebook and began writing in a half-crouched position under the low-hanging branches.

'So are you sure they weren't there before yesterday afternoon?' he asked.

Greg answered for Alex. 'Can't be positive, but I'm pretty sure. It stands to reason though, doesn't it? They've used the dinghy to get the stuff away.'

'In broad daylight?' Jeff poised his pen over the page.

'By water would be less risky than the road. Too risky on our driveway. What if we had returned earlier?'

'You're probably right.' Jeff wrote a little more and, after a firm pen dot to the page, closed his notebook.

'Are you going to fingerprint the boat?' asked Alex.

'We'll try,' responded Marcus, 'although this sort of surface isn't usually very helpful. We'll let it dry off a bit first. So how about we go find this tree hut.' Alex let them lead the way.

As they emerged from the bush into the clearing and the morning sun, a forest of beheaded stalks cast slender shadows across the clearing. Marcus examined the scene. He grunted, shrugged his shoulders, and began gazing among the trees. 'Let's see if I can find this obs. post,' he said.

Noting the blank look on Alex's face, Greg explained. 'Observation post. Your tree hut.'

Jeff moved a little further along the ridge and crouched down before beginning his own search. Alex followed their gaze, occasionally checking the position of the tree hut, but even when they appeared to be looking directly at it, there was no recognition.

Greg whispered, 'Found it.' He nodded carefully in the direction of the pūriri tree. 'Up there among all those plant things.'

Alex smiled. 'Great going, Dad. Why can't Marcus and Jeff see it?'

'Because they are not watching you, are they? I saw how you kept looking there, and that's how I saw it.'

'Cheat,' said Alex with a little laugh.

Greg gave her neck a playful squeeze. 'That's why I'm the detective and they're the constables. Now, how about you save time and show them?'

There were groans, then embarrassed laughs from the two men once she pointed into the pūriri tree. They made their way down to the base of the tree, commenting on how cleverly the obs. post was concealed. Marcus climbed first and peered over the edge of the platform.

'Nothing much here,' he called as he began his cautious descent. He eased himself to the ground, and Jeff immediately took his place, climbing more confidently than his partner. A mixture of bare legs and blue uniform tangled briefly then disappeared over the edge of the platform. Shortly his head poked out.

'Do you want me to throw the rubbish bag down, or should I bring it down with me? It's pretty full.'

'Come on, mate. You can't throw it. We need to take the whole lot to the station for a bit of forensics. You'll have to lower it down if you don't want to fall and smash your fat head open. Is there any cord or something up there?' Jeff disappeared and Marcus waited.

'Tell you what,' came a muffled voice. 'There's a fair bit of old binding twine over the tarpaulin on the roof. I'll try and get it.'

Over the next minutes, there was a lot of movement and noise. Dry ponga fronds and twigs showered down, so they moved back towards the ridge. Here they could more clearly see Jeff, who occasionally leaned out from the platform to reach over the roof. Several times he scrabbled at something, sending another shower of debris to the ground before ducking back out of sight.

'This will have to do.' he called out eventually. His head appeared over the edge. 'Stand by, Marcus. It mightn't be long enough to go all the way.'

A shape teetered briefly and then began its swinging descent. A large black plastic bag came to a swinging halt more than a metre above Marcus, who had moved hurriedly into position, his eyes and arms moving first one way then the other with the bag.

'Jeff,' he called, 'let it go when I say "now".'

'What's that?' asked Jeff.

Marcus repeated the instruction, and immediately, the bag fell with a thud well away from Marcus's reach.

'Not yet, lame brain,' Marcus shouted up the tree.

'You said "now".'

'No, I didn't.'

'Yes, you did. I heard you.'

'No, I was just telling you . . . oh, forget it.'

'What's that?'

Marcus raised his voice tetchily. 'I said "forget it". You'd better come down before that tiny brain of yours collapses completely. Come on.'

Jeff climbed down with surprising agility, a wide grin on his face.

'What about the other things?' Alex called.

'What other things?' Then seeing her look of disbelief, he added, 'There's nothing else up there.'

Marcus had already gathered up the bag and was hauling it back to the waiting group. 'You carry it, young fella,' he said dropping it at Jeff's feet before striding towards the track.

Jeff brought up the rear as they made their way down to the beach. Alex waited for him by the boat shed while the others continued to the bach. Despite the cool morning breeze angling along the shaded sand, beads of perspiration pocked his florid face. Alex indicated to grab one side of the bag.

'Not likely,' he said as he rested to regain his breath. 'I don't want Marcus saying I needed a girl's help. No offence intended,' he added hastily. 'It's just that he's a bit uptight after the bollocking from the sarge. He'll get over it.'

'Jeff, do you think the person in the . . . er, obs. post, would he have done the whole job on his own? Like if it was his crop, would he have planted it, put the camouflage thing over the top, built the obs. post, kept an eye on us, and then cut it all down and taken it away, you know, without anyone else?'

'Not likely. There'll be a group of them. The person in the obs. post must have had a cell phone, and they made arrangements to get it out of there pretty quickly. A bit of a cheek using your dinghy though. Must have left their own one on their mooring.' Jeff heaved the bag over his shoulder and moved on. Alex walked with him.

'There was a heap of marijuana plants up there though, Jeff. It would take a lot of trips down the track, wouldn't it? And they didn't have a whole heap of time really, did they?'

Jeff put the bag down. 'So your question is?'

'Well, it's not a question. It's an idea.' Alex hesitated as her idea gathered shape. 'I honestly don't see how they could cut it, bring it down the track, and take all of it out by our dinghy in the time we were away. It could only take a smallish amount with someone rowing. Do you think they might have hidden some of it somewhere around here and will try to come back for it?'

'Dunno really. Possible, I suppose.' His eyes quickly surveyed the nearby bush. 'Well, that can be another investigation for you, detective constable,' he said with a wry smile. 'Your eyes are sharper than mine. See what you can find.'

They had reached the path up to the bach. A tantalising aroma of frying bacon and toasted bread drew them to the door. Marcus was seated at the table along with Fionna and Samuel, plates of bacon, fried eggs, and tomato in front of them.

'Grab a seat, you two,' said Greg, cracking several eggs into the smoking frying pan. 'It won't be too long.' It was Greg's morning for getting breakfast, and he had insisted on taking over what Fionna had started.

Jeff expressed his thanks and slid in behind the table to sit beside Samuel, their backs to the window. Alex drifted over to the bench.

'Dad, can Samuel and I go out in the dinghy after breakfast? And can we use the outboard motor?' Alex held her breath.

'That's fine,' said Greg as he pulled a tray with grilled bacon and tomatoes from the oven and served it evenly onto three plates. 'Just make sure you wear your life jackets. Where do you want to go?'

'Just around the point, possibly over to Ōponga Bay,' she said casually. 'You know, just stooge around a bit.'

Greg returned for the frying pan and served the eggs. 'OK by me, now grab your plate.' He took Jeff's and his own plate to the table.

After breakfast, Marcus sent Jeff up to their four by four with the rubbish bag and to get the dusting equipment while he enjoyed a second cup of coffee. When he returned, they both went down to fingerprint the dinghy.

Alex caught up with Samuel.

'You were sound asleep this morning,' she said.

'You should have woken me up.'

Alex chose to ignore the edge of complaint in his voice.

'Guess what. All that was left in the hut was a bag of rubbish.' Samuel looked blankly at her. 'Well, don't you think it's strange they were in such a hurry to get the marijuana away but they still bothered to grab cans and bottles of stuff?'

'And the sleeping bag,' Samuel reminded her.

'That too.'

'And the cooker and saucepan.'

'OK. So that's even more stuff they had to take away in such a short time. Samuel, they used our dinghy to get the marijuana out to a launch.'

She paused for dramatic effect. 'But I reckon some of it is hidden around here somewhere.'

Samuel moved as if to immediately begin a search, but she held his arm. 'We can try to find where it's hidden later, but it's more important right now to find the launch because that will lead us to whoever took it. Dad says we can take the dinghy and outboard later on.'

'I know why they took the food and stuff,' Samuel broke in. 'They're poor.'

Her better judgement stopped a contemptuous answer. Instead, she reasoned calmly, 'If they're growing and selling drugs, they won't be poor, Samuel. They grow it because it gets them money. Plenty of money.'

'Then why did they bother taking those things with them?'

The heavy tread of boots on the deck saved her from having to provide an answer she didn't have.

'Not much luck, I'm afraid,' informed Marcus. 'Everything's still too damp, and quite frankly, I don't think we'll get anything worthwhile off it even when it's dry.' Then calling to Greg, he said, 'I'll leave the kit with you. You can drop it into the station next time you're in town. Anyway, we'll be off now. Thanks for the breakfast, Fionna . . . and Greg, of course. That was awesome.'

The train worked its charm on Marcus, who was all smiles once again as the train withdrew steadily up the track. Their sergeant would hopefully be pleased they had some evidence, even if it was all rubbish, as Jeff had reminded him.

Chapter 6

Ōponga

Mum had almost cleared the table, so Alex and Samuel quickly set about washing and drying the dishes and soon had them finished. 'Can we go now, Dad?' Alex asked as her father disappeared through the doorway.

'I was just going to get the outboard motor ready and check the fuel for you,' he called back. 'Grab your hats and life jackets before you come down.'

In a few minutes, the two, with caps on heads and life jackets dangling, burst through the flax and on to the beach. Greg was already dragging the dinghy to the water's edge, and with their eager assistance, it was soon in the water. As he secured the motor to the transom, Fionna wandered down. 'Have fun, you two. And don't do anything I wouldn't do.'

'We will and he won't,' Alex said. She clambered on board after her brother, pleased with the cleverness of her reply.

Greg pushed them into deeper water as she made preparations before pulling sharply on the starter cord. The motor turned but didn't start. After several false starts, the spluttering motor picked up a regular rhythm. A cloud of smoke marked their departure as she opened the throttle and urged the dinghy forward until the hull began to plane smoothly. Samuel turned and grinned at his sister. He signalled thumbs up, then waved at the diminishing figures on the beach as they turned to round the point.

Once around the point, Alex slowed the motor, surveying Jack's Bay, where two yachts and a privately owned, converted tug slumbered. She felt confident none of these looked likely, and as the shallow recesses of Dick's Bay were completely devoid of boats or people, Alex opened the throttle again, steering towards the bush-covered point that protected Ōponga Bay. Rocks jutted at angry angles between the headland and a tiny island from which a single stunted tree sprawled.

'We could go through the gap, Alex,' Samuel suggested, remembering how their father had once navigated a risky passage through those rocks, but that was at high tide. Alex was about to answer when the outline of someone fishing off one of the larger rocks captured her attention. Her suspicion was confirmed as they drew closer. It was that Māori boy. Samuel recognised him at the same time.

'Hey, Alex, look. That's my friend, Hamurara, fishing off that rock.'

'Hā-mu-e-ra, Samuel.' She emphasised each syllable. 'If he's your friend, you'd better get his name right.' She slowed the motor as they approached Hāmuera who, with his back to them, was swinging a hand line in an increasingly fast arc above his head. Just as he was about to release it, Samuel shouted to him. The line looped straight up in the air and plummeted into the water close behind the boy as he fought to regain his balance. He swore loudly, then recognising the occupants of the boat, looked a little abashed.

'Oh, man! Don't do that to me!' he yelled. He began retrieving his line. 'I'm not ready for my own funeral just yet.' His humour had quickly returned.

Alex apologised politely. Samuel asked eagerly, 'Have you caught anything?' The hand line didn't look at all useful.

He didn't answer but shuffled carefully between oyster-covered mounds to retrieve a sack, which he dragged towards himself. He lifted it with both hands. 'Just a few,' he said with dramatic humility. 'Tell you what—it's time I went home for some breakfast. If you fellas give me a lift in your boat, you can have one for yourselves, eh.'

'It's too risky getting in to the rocks there,' Alex called over the idling motor. 'I don't think I can.' She was far from sure she wanted him in the boat with her anyway.

''Course you can. Piri and me, we do it heaps of times. I'll make sure you don't scrape anything. Just come in here where I'm standing, slowly though. You'll see, eh.'

He wound the last of his hand line onto a flax-stalk shaft and sank the fish hooks into its soft ends. Then dragging the sack, he moved carefully forward until he was knee deep in water. 'Come on, then.'

Alex engaged forward gear and steered doubtfully towards Hāmuera. She brought the motor to idle again as the dinghy nosed slowly towards the rocks. In one expert operation, Hāmuera halted its forward motion, hauled the sack on to the bow, planted one knee alongside, and pushed off with his remaining leg. His grin filled the boat. 'See? Not difficult at all. Good driving, Alexandra.' Despite herself, Alex felt a sense of pleasure at his compliment.

It was obvious Hāmuera was used to boats. He moved skilfully from his perch on the bow, placed the sack on the floor, and sat by Samuel. 'OK, captain, take it away,' he said to Alex, with a salute. 'Or should that be first mate?' His eyes teased her above his white-toothed smile.

Alex refused to smile back. 'You'd better tell me where to go if I'm to take it away,' she said. 'I don't know where you live, do I?'

'Ōponga,' he said gesturing with his arm. 'Clear the reef and come round to starboard. I'll show you from there.' He then turned to Samuel and, opening the mouth of the sack, displayed his catch. Samuel was suitably impressed as the two examined the fish and engaged in the conversation of keen fishermen. She had to admit the Māori boy was good with younger children. Maybe he had younger brothers or sisters.

Meanwhile, Alex observed the approaching shoreline. An ancient red tractor connected to a boat trailer and runabout stood at the top of a launching ramp. A number of weather-beaten holiday homes rested among rough patches of grass, and behind them, a wall of bush sloped towards a cloudless sky. She wondered which of the houses was Hāmuera's destination.

As if reading her thoughts, Hāmuera said, 'Our place is further around. Go to the right-hand end of the beach. Watch out though—it gets shallow pretty quickly.'

The bush-covered point was deceptive. The closer they got to the beach, the more it revealed another small cove nestled back where the point began jutting into the sea. An old launch with peeling paint sat at an uneasy angle where the ebbing tide had left it almost clear of the water. Alex slowed the motor to a crawl and raised it so the propeller, while still in the water, was clear of the muddy seabed. When they were almost abreast of the launch, Hāmuera said, 'Better stop the motor now, Alexandra.'

How? Alex fumbled for a switch. In growing panic, she stood up to search the other side of the motor, and instantly, the dinghy tipped, almost toppling her into the water. The propeller came clear of the water and with it, the loudly popping exhaust. The next moment, there was a yell followed by a splash as Hāmuera went over the side still gripping the boat with one hand where he had been about to step out. His shoulder and head remained clear, but everything else went under as he fell sideways into the shallow water.

'Alex!' Samuel yelled. 'What did you do that for?'

The exhaust continued to pop noisily, adding to her confusion. Alex dropped the propeller back into the water, but because it was still in gear, it dug into the mud and the motor stalled. With ears pounding and eyes filling, she battled to regain her balance and her composure.

'I'm sorry,' she wailed, and then with genuine concern, she asked, 'Are you all right, Hāmuera?'

Hāmuera sat in the water, his head thrown back and his mouth wide open. Instead of a cry of anguish, he began to hoot. Tears of laughter became indistinguishable from the streaks of seawater on his face. Samuel joined him, then Alex who, as much from relief as from his infectious laughter, could not restrain herself.

Hāmuera stood up, his saturated clothes clinging to his body. 'Oh, man,' he roared, trying to keep a stern face. 'That was wicked, Alexandra! You don't have to tip me out because you don't like me.' Laughter welled up again.

'I didn't do it deliberately, it was an accident, and I do like you.' The silence that followed lasted an eternity as Alex tried to rescue herself from what she had just said. 'I mean, I don't hate you or anything . . . I—'

It was Hāmuera who rescued the situation. 'Hey, I said we could be friends didn't I? No big deal.' He was not teasing her this time. A serious expression chased the laughter lines across his face. He slapped his hands against his wet thighs, breaking the moment of awkwardness. 'Well, I'd better get home and get out of these, eh.'

He reached into the dinghy and, after searching briefly in the sack, pulled out two pan-sized snapper. 'There's a fillet of fish for you fellas.'

'I can't take those,' Alex began, but Samuel assured the Māori boy they could. 'Thank you,' she said lamely. 'Thank you very much, especially after what I've done to you. I really am very sorry.'

'Forget it,' he said, a wide grin stretching across his face again. He lifted his sack from the dinghy and waited until Alex had lifted the propeller shaft out of the mud before giving the boat a good shove back into deeper water. 'See you 'round,' he said with a casual wave before turning and wading towards the shore.

Alex pulled on the starter cord and was relieved when it came to life immediately. For several minutes, she was busy reversing, periodically tilting the propeller shaft when it stirred up mud. Finally, confident they were out of the shallows, she looked back to the beach just in time to see Hāmuera disappearing into a small opening in the shoreline scrub. Her eyes traced an imaginary path through the trees above the opening. Then she saw it, a barely discernible snatch of rusty red roof nestled among tall kānuka and ponga tree fronds almost halfway up the slope. So that was where he stayed.

A land breeze had begun to ruffle the water, and the ride was rougher now as she pointed towards Ōrokawa. Samuel sat with his back to the bow, contentedly looking at their wake, perhaps dreaming of fishing with Hāmuera. The boy had distracted her from her main purpose, but there was promise in the number of craft at anchor ahead.

She weaved slowly among the boats. Several yachts ghosted silently past their neighbours with the arrival of the breeze. Orange buoys bobbed and nodded where they had slipped their moorings. The promise was greater than the reality, however. Most of the boats displayed children or old folk, which raised little suspicion, and none looked vaguely like vehicles for crime. Just how she would recognise a suspicious boat was unclear, but deep inside, she was confident she would.

Samuel was becoming impatient. 'Let's go back, Alex,' he said, shifting uncomfortably on the seat. 'This is boring and I've got a numb bum.'

'Soon,' she said. 'Just a bit longer. You should be looking too, Samuel. We're solving this one together, remember?' She hoped his involvement in the search might buy her time. It didn't work.

'I *have* been looking,' he protested testily.

Warning signs began flashing. Intuitively, Alex said, 'I need a rest from steering. Would you like to have a go?' Instantly the signs stopped flashing.

'Really? Yes, please!'

Alex brought the motor to idle, and they carefully exchanged places. For the second time that day, a smile filled the boat. After an unsteady start, he mastered the tiller, and apart from occasionally giving a hand signal to direct his course, Alex gave all her attention to examining the remaining craft.

By the time they approached the western end of the Ōrokawa beach, boats were widely spread, and it was clear their search had been fruitless. Disappointed, she pointed to the cliffs at the end of the beach and gave Samuel the thumbs-up sign when he opened the throttle.

Despite the bumpy ride over the mounting waves, she reviewed her thinking. *To get the marijuana away in such a hurry, they used this dinghy to transport it out to a bigger craft that couldn't come too close to shore. It has to be a launch, doesn't it? And because they had to do everything in such a short time, that launch must have been quite nearby, certainly no further away than Ōrokawa.*

So it has to be somewhere in the bay, surely. But hold on a minute, just because it was nearby doesn't mean it has stayed in the bay after getting the stuff, does it? It could have left and gone straight off to . . . just about anywhere.

She inspected the expanse of sea between Tāpeka Point in the distance and the closer features of Roberton Island. Many craft dotted the water, but all were too far off to make out any significant detail. It was a lost cause.

I wouldn't have wasted all this time if I had thought a bit smarter. Still, if I'm right about them hiding some of it back at the beach, there's a chance we can get on their trail again. Anyway, it's been pleasant enough nosing around the bay. And Hāmuera . . .

Her eyes were unseeing, but she saw it in her mind; it really was funny—now—about Hāmuera falling in the water. The look on his face. And that laugh. And his clothes wringing wet. He really had been very forgiving. And generous with the fish he had caught.

'What are you smiling about?' Samuel's voice intruded.

'Nothing. Nothing really. Well, actually I was thinking about Hāmuera,' she confided.

'Yeah, he's a good fisherman, all right, isn't he?'

'Yes, just what I was thinking,' she replied, allowing another smile to escape.

Their beach was just coming into view, so Samuel was happy enough to exchange places and let his sister take back the controls. She did not see the launch hugging the far side of Manawaora Bay, its flared bow cutting a thin white passage through the water towards Pāroa Bay.

Chapter 7

Crab and Conscience

The afternoon proved just as fruitless as the morning. After lunch, Samuel had started off with good intentions, but he soon became bored and had gone to look for crabs around the rocks. Alex didn't blame him because each place they had searched revealed no hidden marijuana. Like Pooh Bear, the more they looked, the more it wasn't there.

Grey clouds had closed the day in, and Alex was feeling quite disconsolate when she abandoned her search and returned to the bach later that afternoon. Greg arrived at the same time. The handyman had finished replacing the smashed panels with armoured glass, and installed a new lockable handle and deadlock on the front door of the house. Permanent replacements for his temporary repairs made Greg feel much better, and when Gran and Grandpa arrived, they would be more secure, he said.

With all the recent events, she had completely forgotten they were arriving for New Year's Eve, and this thought lifted her spirits a little. She knew they would listen to every detail of the happenings. Gran really understood her feelings, yet she was very practical about dealing with them. And Grandpa seemed to know something about almost everything. He would probably want to search with her, which was fine, as long as they didn't get sidetracked. He loved to point out things and teach her about them. As Mum said, 'He's a retired teacher who hasn't tired of teaching.' Alex was almost certain she could find the marijuana—if it was still around, if it was there in the first place. She had to admit that was a possibility.

'It's a shame, but I think there's a turn in the weather,' Greg said, looking thoughtfully out the seaward windows. 'Could be raining tomorrow.'

'What a shame after the beautiful morning we had,' Fionna said. 'Still, it won't hurt to have a rest from the sun,' She came a little closer to Alex. 'Yes, I thought you looked a bit burnt on the top of your arms. Oh, and look at your nose! You must use your sunscreen, Alex, especially when you are out on the water.'

'I'm OK, Mum. It doesn't hurt,' she replied, trying to ignore the suspicious tightness in her skin.

Samuel's footsteps pounded along the deck. Bursting through the door, he said, 'Look at this.' Then stirring a two-litre ice-cream container with a stick, he enthused, 'That's the biggest one we've ever found, isn't it?'

A crusty purple-and-white claw grasped the stick, and a sizeable crab grappled the air as he proudly raised it, suspended by one claw. Its tiny mouth foamed in impotent fury.

'Samuel, don't be so cruel.' Samuel caught the hint of fear in her tone. He menaced towards her, and the crab wobbled precariously on the stick.

'It won't hurt you, Alex,' he teased. 'Look.'

'No, Samuel, don't!' she said, trying to quell her panic.

'Samuel,' Greg warned. But Samuel was enjoying his sister's reaction. He kept approaching her slowly as she backed towards her bunk.

'Samuel!' The edge in Greg's voice should have been sufficient, but Samuel was heedless of subtleties now. With a tormenting leer, he thrust the stick towards her. At that very moment, the crab released the stick, and Alex saw it in slow motion, floating through the air towards her bunk. It hit the edge of the bed and then, in real time, fell to the floor. For one stunned moment, it remained unmoving before scuttling along the floorboards and into dark refuge under the bunks.

Alex was startled by a prolonged, piercing scream. It stopped the instant she gasped for breath. Things happened quickly after that. The plastic container fell to the floor. Fionna shrieked. Samuel was ushered out the door in Greg's firm grip. Outside, Greg yelled and Samuel wailed, 'No, Daddy!' followed by falsetto cries of sudden pain. Fionna leapt forward to shovel the spill of aquatic creatures back into the container with the dustpan, and Alex found herself on a top bunk, without remembering how she got there.

Greg left Samuel wailing outside, and although nothing was said, Alex sensed that events outside upset her mother more than the crab under the bed and the mess on the floor. Greg picked up on it also.

'He can come inside when he's calmed down and is ready to apologise,' he said stiffly, and taking the torch from the top of the chest of drawers, he began searching under the bunk for the crab. He found it backed into the farthest recess, claws at the ready to defend itself. Shortly, he returned the torch and sat at the table, his back to the kitchen bench. 'I'm not going in there. He can get it himself,' he said.

'Can't you reach it?' Fionna asked. The question sounded like a challenge. She paused, then added, 'I'll get it, then.'

Greg turned, and there was a strained moment before he said firmly, 'I can get it all right. It's not as if it's a weta.'

He never disguised his revulsion of that large and repulsive bush insect. 'Samuel dropped it—he can get it back. That's what I mean,' he said with finality.

Just then, the door opened slowly, and Samuel stood, tear-stained and red-faced, looking in.

Fionna coached him through an apology for scaring his sister and for disobedience, but when Greg told him to go under the bunks and retrieve the crab, he was suddenly tearful again. He seemed spooked by the incident, and despite everything, Alex began to feel sorry for him as he backed against the door, resisting every encouragement to take the torch and at least look for it.

Alex slid off the bunks, and barely controlling the panic that threatened to overwhelm her, she took the dustpan and instructed her brother. 'You hold the torch, and I'll try to scoop it into this.' She knelt before the bunks. 'Come on. I can't hold the torch *and* scoop it up, Samuel. I need you to help.'

Samuel moved reluctantly, but once the torch beam located it, he became animated. 'There he is. I can see him. He's not very happy, is he? I'll get him, Alex.'

But Alex had something to prove to herself. She ignored his offer and, with the pan extended before her, wriggled on her stomach into a better position. Samuel kept the torch focussed on the crab. The pan touched its front legs, and the creature raised its claws defensively. She paused for her courage to return, then edged the pan carefully forward. Suddenly it scuttled on to the pan and threatened to crawl right over the back lip by the handle. Instinctively, Alex withdrew her hand. Her head connected with the wooden bunk frame above, and she let out a sharp cry.

Instantly, Greg was alongside, comforting her as she rubbed the painful swelling. Meanwhile, Samuel reached in and withdrew the dustpan. Sensing freedom lay in a different direction, the crab cleared the side of the pan and skittered and scratched swiftly across the floor towards Fionna who, with adrenalin-fuelled speed, dropped a beach towel over it. She retreated to the bed divan while the crustacean struggled valiantly to escape. Finally it conceded victory to the starfish-and-stripes towel and lay still.

Samuel, no longer spooked, held the crab in position with one hand and pulled back the towel with the other. Mum watched from a respectful distance, offering small cautionary instructions. He gripped the crab firmly across its back then held it aloft. Greg and Alex moved aside as he marched triumphantly to the doorway.

'He's saying, "Gotta go now, see ya later."' Its limbs scrabbled at the air. Then he was gone.

Fionna and Greg looked at each other with that coded look parents use when a child is present. But Alex was no longer a child, and she correctly interpreted it as *that needed seriousness, so keep a straight face, but wasn't it hilarious as well?*

She was far from sure she agreed. It had been a truly frightening experience, and as she allowed herself to relive the moments, her scalp began to crawl and her spine quiver. But at least she had learned she could control fear when she really tried. She gingerly felt the bump on her head.

Her book didn't want to be read. Every time she opened it, the words disappeared, and her own story, more like a movie than a story, took their place. It was hopeless. And then Samuel was calling her from the beach.

'What?' she yelled back from her bunk.

'Alex, don't just shout. Go and see what he wants,' Fionna instructed.

'Well, he's shouting at me, isn't he?'

'Do as your mother says.' Greg was having none of this. 'He's outside, you're inside. There's a difference.'

Not daring to argue further, she stomped heavily to the door, ignorant of her parents' arched eyebrows. She closed the door more firmly than needed and marched along the wooden deck. Greg shrugged his shoulders at Fionna, grinned, and suggested they have a cup of tea.

Samuel was waiting for her just beyond the flax bushes.

'What?' she repeated.

'I've got something to show you.' he said excitedly. 'It's along by the boat shed.'

'I'm not interested, Samuel. The last thing you showed me gave me a bump on the head, and I'm not happy with you.' She turned back towards the flax.

Samuel was undeterred. 'I'm sorry about your head. Truly. But you do need to see this. Alexandra, please,' he pleaded as she began to press back through the opening.

This use of her name surprised her. She couldn't remember the last time he had called her by her full name. She turned to face him.

'It had better be good, Samuel.' She hesitated. 'If this is another silly trick of yours, you'd better watch out, because right now I don't like you very much.'

'No, it's not anything like that. Come on.'

He turned and walked quickly towards the boat shed without glancing back. He was confident she would follow. His sincerity, enthusiasm, and faith in her made him difficult to ignore, so she trudged after him. He didn't stop until he reached the boat shed. There he turned and waited for her.

'OK, now what is it?' she demanded.

He beckoned for her to follow him behind the shed. *He's found the marijuana, the clever little beggar.*

'Hi, Alexandra.'

The voice made her jump. Hāmuera stood before her.

'Didn't Samuel tell you?'

She looked sharply at her brother, who was grinning from ear to ear. 'No, he didn't, and actually I've had enough frights for one day, thank you very much. What are you doing here?'

'I asked Samuel, but he said you had to give me permission.'

'Permission? What for?'

'I need to borrow your dinghy tonight. I don't think your parents will be keen for that, but you can trust me, so how about it?'

'They won't, you're right. What do you need it for?'

'To visit my nana, over there.' He waved vaguely beyond the boat shed.

'At night?'

'It's the only time I got, eh.'

She looked long and hard at the boy before speaking. 'And why don't you drive there? It's quicker and easier, isn't it?'

His gaze shifted back and forth between the girl and her brother. A smile tweaked his lips. 'I haven't got my driver's licence yet,' he quipped. Then quickly reading her face, he added, 'Actually, Piri could make a lot of trouble if he found out. He doesn't like me having anything to do with her. Something about she doesn't like his mates with their Harleys and booze and all that. He won't know if I row there at night, will he? He'll just think I'm out fishing again.'

'How long would you need it for?'

'I don't know. Maybe three or four hours. It will be back in the morning. No one will know—except for you two, eh. So how about it?'

Remembering his generous gift of fish earlier in the day made it difficult for her to turn down his request without seeming extremely mean-spirited.

'I guess,' she sighed. 'But if you make any noise and they catch you, don't you bring me into it.'

Hāmuera had been very grateful, and Samuel told her she was a very kind person as she strode ahead of him back to the bach.

Everyone was preparing for bed. The usual gentle lapping of waves on the beach had become noisier with the approaching wild weather. Dad said he was glad he had put the runabout back in the boat shed for the night, but he had clean forgotten to pull the dinghy higher up into the flax. He was pleased when Alex hastily said she would do it, but not half as much as Alex.

The dinghy was already gone. Awkward questions would be asked if the boat was not there in the morning. Nagging guilt over deceiving her parents began to push the boy's gratefulness and her brother's kind words into a dark hole.

As she lay in bed, gusts of wind scraped branches outside the wall beside her. Her earnest prayers were for the boat's safe return, and the boy, of course.

Chapter 8

After the Storm

When daylight came, the dinghy lay across the morning-grey rocks like a great sea elephant, motionless above the sucking tide and furtive crabs. Alex eyed it from the vast line of shells heaped above the high-water mark by the pounding waves during the night.

A lone seagull performed a silent arc and skittered on to rocks beside the dinghy, eyeing it cautiously before stepping closer. Alex knew there was a lot of explaining to do and a lot of trouble if she gave away anything that connected this with Hāmuera. The seagull made a short dash to the boat and then, with one flap of its wings, settled upon its upturned hull. A few shakes and it settled its wings neatly against its body, warily cocking its head this way and that. She needed the same caution if her father was not to suspect anything.

She made her way over the heaped stones and the bedrock exposed by the crashing waves, glad for the diving shoes she had pulled on.

'Alex!' Samuel's stage whisper was throaty and anxious.

She paused and let her brother catch up.

'What are we going to tell Mum and Dad?' he rasped, his eyes continuing to absorb the scene.

Alex didn't answer. They hurried in concentrated silence, picking their way among the oyster-covered rocks to where the dinghy lay. The seagull waited until the last moment before stirring its wings to flutter a small distance away, where it adopted a watchful posture.

At first glance, there appeared to be little damage. The upturned bow lay on a sprawling pōhutukawa bough that see-sawed just above the rocks. Its stern was wedged into the opening of a small crease lined with sea snails and barnacles. They walked slowly around the boat examining it for any sign of punctured aluminium.

'There's only this deep scratch down near the stern and no holes anywhere,' Alex said with relief. 'Once it's in the water, no one will notice it. Here, you grab the bow and I'll lift the stern.'

Together they raised the dinghy and, at Alex's command, strained their way towards a miniature inlet between two rocky outcrops, Alex moving backward with careful glances over her shoulder and Samuel forward, but unable to see where to place his feet. Although heavy, it was manageable, and before long, their ungainly progress brought them to the water's edge.

'Right, let's turn it over. One, two, three,' Alex counted.

The bow twisted out of Samuel's grip and fell right side up with a crunching thud. The seagull flapped its wings and quickly departed.

'Careful!' Alex scowled, with a quick look in the direction of the bach. 'We don't need Mum or Dad to hear.'

'I didn't mean to!' said Samuel, his pitch rising with indignation. Alex ignored his response, and after she signalled him to lift it again, it was soon floating in the water. She clambered quickly aboard.

'Oh, no!' she gasped. 'Where's the oars?'

For a moment, they looked at each other. The oars could be anywhere. They could be floating out to sea, wedged in rocks around the point, or spread along the shoreline as barely recognisable splinters of wood.

After a thoughtful pause, Alex said, 'Samuel, I'll go around the rocks this way and have a good look for the oars. You tow this around to the beach before Mum and Dad get suspicious. Keep your eyes wide open . . . and your mind on the job,' she added.

Samuel narrowed his eyes but didn't reply. His parents often used the phrase—for good reason. He waded back towards the beach, towing the salvaged dinghy in the shallows close to the rocks.

Everything in the bay slept in exhaustion. High cloud shielded the early morning sun. A silver sheen blanketed the sea beyond the inner islands/and out to the open ocean. Water gently licked the rocks near Alex's feet, advancing and retreating with the barest smacking of its lips. The tide was on the wane, which was helpful. Wind-lashed waves might have washed any floating object above high water.

Alex picked her way among the familiar rocks, her eyes searching for shapes in the flotsam that would announce the end of her search. There was a freshly wrenched branch, spikes of old driftwood, a fence batten, and fragments of painted planking from a dead boat, mingled with kelp, plastic bags, several lemon skins, a faded pink plastic clothes peg, and strings of King Neptune's necklace.

The distant deep throb of a diesel engine slid across the water as a lone yacht, curling a white bow wave, rounded the small island at the end of

Ōrokawa peninsula. All craft had left Ōrokawa the previous afternoon for shelter from the forecast southerly. Now the first of many was returning for protection from ocean swell and the prevailing nor'wester winds. By evening, there would be a forest of masts again, their masthead lights languidly rocking among the stars on the northern horizon.

Approaching a sprawling rocky outcrop where fishermen occasionally cast their lines, she spied a human silhouette dancing awkwardly against the backlit sky. The figure seemed to leap, hover, shrink, and advance, its arms flailing the air as if beating off angry hornets. Alex paused and watched its progress with a mixture of curiosity and apprehension. Gradually her curiosity turned to recognition.

'Hāmuera!' she called out. 'What's up?'

The dancer continued his awkward rock running until he came closer.

'These damn, dumb rocks are cutting my feet to bits.'

He selected a small area of smoother rock, sat down, and carefully inspected the soles of each foot.

'Man, they sting!' He looked up. 'What are you doing out here so early, Alexandra?'

Alex decided there was a far more important question that needed answering. 'Did you change your mind? You said you were going to your nana's place,' she insisted.

Hāmuera's face was impassive, but his eyes betrayed discomfort.

'Yeah, that's right.' He took a slow, deep breath and gazed without focus up the cliff face. 'That's what I did. I rowed 'round to Pāroa Bay, and I saw her. She was real happy to see me. She cooked up some kai, and we had a cup of tea and a good long kōrerō. Everything's good . . . ka pai.' His head nodded firmly to confirm the last point.

'Everything's not good with our dinghy.' Alex paused, searching the Māori boy's face. 'I found it on the rocks this morning. You're lucky it wasn't more badly damaged. And the oars have gone,' she added. 'I'm trying to find them before Dad finds out.'

'They're up the side of the boat shed.'

'What?' Alex narrowed her eyes. 'Come on, Hāmuera. What's going on?'

'Nothing's going on. I told you what I did.'

In a low and measured voice, she said, 'When the wind got up last night, I told Dad I would check the dinghy was all right with the weather turning rough, and stuff. It was about nine o'clock when I came down to the beach, and you weren't back then. When I got back into bed, the storm really got going. I was worried you wouldn't get back in time. I guessed you would stay at your nana's until the storm stopped and then try to get back.'

'Yeah, that's what I did. And I got up early this morning once the calm came, and I rowed it back and put the oars . . . ' His voice slowed and stopped.

'And you put the oars up beside the boat shed,' continued Alex, 'then hauled the dinghy up over the rocks and forced it upside down onto a pōhutukawa branch without making any noise all on your own? Yeah, right!'

Hāmuera looked solemn and his jaw clenched and unclenched. Slowly his eyes began to twinkle.

'You sure got me there. For a minute, I thought you didn't believe me. Now I will have to reveal to you my true identity, but you have to promise never to reveal it to another living soul, eh.'

He stood to his feet, broadened his chest, and jutted out his chin. 'My true identity is . . . Hāmuera the Māori Marvel. I put on my great grandfather's korowai, and instantly, I have powers. I fly through the air without wings. I swim deep in the sea without needing to breathe. I lift huge weights, such as my cousin Piri, and . . . I can read your thoughts.' A barely perceptible quiver tugged at the corners of his mouth.

'Go on, then.'

'You are thinking . . . everything I told you is a lie, eh?' He sat down again.

For a moment, the two looked at each other. Finally their laughter could be held back no longer. Alex shook her head and said, 'Man, you can tell lies.'

'I don't tell lies,' protested Hāmuera with mock severity. 'I tell imaginations.' After a short pause he said, 'Actually, I was coming to find your boat.'

There was a different tone in his voice now, which suggested the truth was finally coming. 'I can't tell you what I needed your boat for because it could get me and someone else in real big trouble. And you're right. I didn't go to Nana's.' Alex drew a breath to speak, but her friend broke in, 'No, don't ask me where I went. If I told you, I'd have to kill you, eh.'

Noting the instant alarm on Alex's face, he assured her, 'It's just a saying.' Alex nodded, but wasn't fully convinced. 'Sorry, Alexandra, but it's better you don't know, then you can't let it slip by accident. Trust me.'

Alex tried a different tack. 'Where did you come from this morning? You must've been up pretty early. It's not even half past six yet.'

Hāmuera stood up and took a few careful steps to a higher position on the rocks. 'If you've found the dinghy, I'll head back. Sorry about how you found it, and that . . . you know,' he added awkwardly.

Alex nodded. 'That's OK. It's good you're all right. See you.'

She watched as Hāmuera hopped and hobbled his way over the rocks, his arms flailing the air as he fought for his balance. A sudden thought crossed her mind. 'Where are your shoes, Hāmuera?' she yelled.

Hāmuera appeared not to have heard. There was no pause as his diminishing figure continued on its comical way, and at the very moment he rounded the point, sun pierced the morning cloud, instantly turning the seawater aquamarine. It was going to be a great day.

The oars now safely stowed where they belonged, Alex tried to look casual as she came off the wooden slatted deck and into the bach. Fionna was preparing breakfast at the kitchen bench. Greg was busily sweeping the floor and shaping a small pile of sand ready for the hand broom and pan. With the beach a mere ten metres from the bach, it was inevitable that sand would be brought inside despite the plastic foot bath at the door in which everyone was meant to dip their feet. She skirted around the busy sweeper, relieved that neither seemed to note her entry and there was no need to face questioning.

Samuel sat on the edge of his bunk, a book on his knees, but his eyes asked the question, *Have you found the oars?* She gave a little shrug as if to say, *No, couldn't find them,* then noticing the instant dismay on her brother's face, decided to be kind and gave a nod followed by a wink.

'You were both up early.' Mum's voice startled her. 'The noisy weather last night obviously didn't keep you two awake.' The frying pan spluttered as an egg slid into the smoking oil.

'What's the beach like? Much seaweed thrown up?' Dad inquired.

'Heaps. Quite a bit of that King Neptune's necklace stuff,' Alex offered. 'Quite a bit of driftwood too.' She tried to not catch Samuel's eye.

Following a brief pause as he stored the hand broom and pan away, Dad added, 'I hope our boat's OK. You checked on the dinghy before bed, didn't you, Alex? Everything all right this morning?'

For a moment, her mind became a summer whirlwind whisking thoughts like leaves in a revolving frenzy. Then an image of the seagull on the upturned hull cautiously cocking its head appeared, and abruptly, the whirlwind ceased. *Dad wants to know if everything is all right this morning. Of course it is . . . now.*

'Yeah, everything's good this morning. The cicadas are singing,' Alex added, and sensing Samuel's eyes on her, she affirmed what her inner voice had earlier announced: 'And it's going to be a great day.'

Chapter 9

Trespassers

Down on the beach after breakfast, Samuel questioned Alex with intensity, his eyes begging for an answer. 'What did Hāmuera do with our boat?'

'Dunno,' Alex replied. Hāmuera had given her no genuine information. She gazed out over the water, deep in thought, not actually seeing anything.

'Well, he nearly wrecked it—that's what he did,' her brother continued.

Alex didn't answer. She briefly considered giving her brother an account of her conversation with Hāmuera before deciding there wasn't a lot to be gained by doing so. The boy had revealed nothing. Then remembering the most chilling part, she told him, 'He said he would have to kill me if he told me.' She enjoyed the look on her brother's face as he recoiled.

'Hāmuera said that?' His voice rose in a mixture of disbelief and anxiety. 'He wouldn't do that. Would he?'

'Nah. He was kidding.' Her voice trailed off. Her eyes spotted and followed a jet ski rounding the point, a white rooster tail of water spouting behind it. Above its mosquito whine, she said, 'I think he would like to tell us but he's a bit scared.'

'Would either of you like to come fishing?' Greg's voice interrupted. In an instant, Samuel was on his feet.

'Yes, please!'

Greg was already untying the cord that secured the dinghy to the kowhai tree and had begun hauling the bow around, ready to drag it to the water's edge. Alex joined her brother in an instant. 'We'll do it, Dad,' she offered.

'That was close,' she muttered as the two pulled the dinghy in noisy scrapings over the pebbly sand. They didn't want any chance of their father noticing the damage and asking awkward questions about last night.

Fionna came down to check they had their life jackets on and to see them off with a pack of food and drink.

'I've taken some sausages out of the freezer for tonight, but if you catch anything, we can have them tomorrow night. I'm putting in my order for another pan-sized snapper. OK?'

Her encouragement worked on Samuel, who confidently promised to bring her more than one back.

Before long, rods and bait had been stowed, the fifteen-horsepower outboard motor was attached to the transom, and Dad was tugging at the starter cord. It was a reluctant starter.

'We could take *Scoot*.' Samuel looked hopefully in the direction of the boat shed tucked into the bush and almost invisible behind the low boughs of the ancient pōhutukawa tree.

'No. We'll keep fish smells for our dinghy. Anyway, there's not enough petrol left. I'm going into Russell tomorrow to get the tanks filled. We can take *Scoot* once we have full tanks.'

The red plastic fuel tanks often sat in the back of the station wagon on their trips into town. Fifty litres didn't last too many days running *Scoot*'s sixty-five-horsepower outboard motor.

After a little tinkering with the choke, the small motor screamed into life before settling down to Greg's hasty throttle adjustment. Both children were glad for their father's close attention to the motor. It took away the likelihood of him noticing any signs of recent damage.

'We won't go too far,' Greg said. 'They say that after a bit of a blow and some rain, the fish come in close. Mind you,' he added, 'they say the opposite too. Who knows?'

He turned the tiller handle until the bow pointed towards Tāpeka Point in the distance before twisting the throttle wide open. The boat struggled to get up to planing speed, so Alex moved carefully aft, where Samuel sat with the motor between him and their father. As soon as the dinghy picked up speed, Alex returned to the centre seat and sat facing the bow, turning her head until the wind arranged her hair off her face. Vibrations juddered the hull, tickling the soles of her bare feet. Misted spray glittered on her bare arms.

Man, this is the life . . . just love this sun and sea and sand and stuff. Who needs school? Wonder what Nicole's doing, not going away anywhere . . . mother has to keep working, father away on business or something . . . Laura's up here somewhere . . . might run into her, probably in Russell, maybe Paihia. We might get a launch . . . Dad thinks the runabout is a bit small to go out to where the big ones are . . . sunbathe on the foredeck, dive off the flying bridge . . . man, I love this place.

Alex became aware of the jet ski some distance from their port beam. It was performing tight circles at high speed, throwing up walls of spray and bringing the craft to a swirling halt that threatened to unseat the rider.

She watched with detached interest until it came closer and she was able to see both rider and machine more clearly. The white jet ski was adorned with fluorescent red stripes edged by orange and yellow flame streaks. The rider gunned the throttle, and it rose from the sea like a hooked marlin. It leapt forward, turned, and passed at high speed, its motor shrieking, across their bow.

It was then that Alex recognised the rider. His large torso was bare. Thick tattooed arms extended from broad shoulders to grip the steering bar. An enormous backside and thigh were squeezed into voluminous Hawaiian board shorts, and a sturdy leg anchored him to the ski. His bearded face turned briefly to gauge the distance from the dinghy. It was Hāmuera's cousin.

And then he was gone, a curved line of spray tracing his path towards Ōponga Bay until he disappeared around Dick's Point. Before Dad could throttle back, the dinghy hit its wake. Spray showered from the tossing bow as everyone held on tight.

Greg was annoyed. He throttled right back. 'What is it with these Māori? Think they own the place. Don't give a thought for others. I bet he doesn't know the first thing about rules on the water. They're as bad on the water as they are on the road.'

Alex thought that was a bit unfair. Surprisingly, Greg hadn't made the connection between that driver and this rider. Nor had Samuel when they talked about it later. But it was Samuel who, still unconvinced, asked the question.

'If that *was* him, how come he's got a flash jet ski when his car is an old bomb?'

They had gone into the sheltered waters of Pāroa Bay because Greg felt sure the loose formation of terns flying beyond the headland meant sprats were schooling and where there are sprats, there are larger fish herding them into meal-sized groups. Kahawai first, then snapper below them and with luck, kingfish happy to flash through all layers for anything their mouths can snatch, even baited hooks or spinner lures.

Samuel was impatient, and each time their lines had been let down and no bites were felt within a few minutes, he pleaded with his father to move to another spot. He was very patient fishing familiar places, but today there was no time to waste on unrewarding waters.

Finally, Greg gave up trying to follow the excitedly wheeling and diving birds. They flapped quickly away, skimming waves to join yet another squawking flock, circling, aborting dives, or hovering skilfully above the surface.

A spot close to a small reef barely covered by high tide showed promise, as almost immediately there were strong tugs on their lines. Greg's rod shuddered strongly, and he began to reel in. Shortly a silvery dart sliced from side to side beneath the surface. Before Greg could bring it to the surface, Samuel shouted, 'Got one!' and he began reeling in with a determined grin on his face.

Over the next fifteen minutes, Alex watched as the two reeled fish after fish into the boat. Most were not keepers, but the fish bag contained five pan-sized snapper by the time she felt her rod yank.

'Got one too!' she called excitedly. Greg was cutting up some mackerel for bait.

'About time,' he teased. 'I thought you'd just come along for the ride.'

The line went slack, and for a disappointing moment, Alex thought her fish had slipped the hook. Then the rod almost pulled from her hand as the nylon line twanged. Greg looked up with renewed interest. Samuel was instantly alert.

'Wow!' he exclaimed. 'That's a big one. Don't let it get off.'

Over the next minutes, Alex steadily wound in her line, ignoring the advice her brother offered. She knew she was winning even when she released the line tension several times to play her fish. When finally it came close enough to the surface, Greg announced, 'Looks like a kingie. Get the landing net, Samuel.'

Samuel pulled it from the anchor shelf and handed it to his father before taking a position to peer over the side.

'There it is,' he said, pointing. 'It's a kingie all right!'

It wasn't as big as she had thought, even underwater, which tended to magnify size and give rise to fishermen's tales, but it definitely was a kingfish, all sleek and silver and strong.

As she lifted it from the water for her father to slip the landing net under, she glimpsed a small kahawai in the kingfish's mouth. This sometimes happened when the desperate threshing of a hooked fish attracts a predator, which also gets snagged by the same hook.

The kingfish fought vigorously without the water's support. Greg leaned over the side, stretching to get its tail inside the hoop, but at the crucial moment, it wriggled furiously, flopped off the hook, teetered momentarily on the rim and plopped back into the sea despite his desperate efforts. It briefly gathered its bearings and then with a flick of its tail dived and was gone.

For a moment, everyone was silent. Then Alex said, 'Nearly.'

'I'm sorry,' Greg said. 'Too bad.'

Samuel said nothing, but when they had nearly got back to Clendon Point, he said, 'You can have one of mine, Alex. I don't need them all.'

She grinned at him. 'Thanks. Better luck next time, eh?'

'Yeah,' he replied, 'better luck next time.'

Freshly caught fish grilled over driftwood embers is heavenly. On a late December evening with the sun setting over a tranquil New Zealand beach, it is paradise. A smudge of woodsmoke climbed the rock face and disappeared into the vivid green foliage above. Wisps of cloud flushed pink as the sun nestled into the coastal hills. Now that the breeze had died and the water calmed, cicadas serenaded the entire beach.

In the late afternoon, before the fishing expedition had landed, Fionna had brought the beach furniture to their favourite spot. She listened with interest as the children recounted the events of the afternoon and applauded their catch. She sympathised with Alex over the big one that got away.

'But I said she can have one of mine,' said Samuel, withdrawing his hand from the plastic bag and holding up one of the smaller fish as proof. Fionna commended Samuel for his generosity.

Alex smiled ruefully. *It's the thought that counts.*

Her parents sat on familiar white plastic chairs, their faces bathed in the golden glow of the setting sun, sipping cool drinks. They held them loosely in day's-end hands and talked quietly together. At other times, they turned to stare contentedly across the water, through eyes half closed against the red glare.

Samuel had gravitated to the rocks and was busy inspecting the few remaining crab crevices before the incoming tide swamped them. Alex watched him idly. Beyond his bobbing form, the broad stretch of Manawaora Farm rose above the pipi beds that stretched from the mangroves to the large shed at the other end of Farm Beach.

The last time they had gone to gather pipis from the muddy sand, she had gone quite silly after Samuel had tossed a small crab at her. Up to that moment, the thought of crabs had not entered her head. After that, every squelching step had made her shoulders hunch in dread of nasty, nipping creatures somewhere under her feet.

Samuel had suffered a badly upset stomach that same night, and Dad said it might be run-off from the farm contaminating the shellfish. It was strange then that Samuel was the only one who became ill, because they had all eaten some. Alex was nevertheless grateful they hadn't returned since. Pipis were nice to eat—if someone else gathered them.

Samuel stood up, and as her eyes flicked towards him, Alex caught another movement behind. A car was driving slowly from the distant boat shed. Even at that distance, she recognised it as the battered brown car belonging to Hāmuera's cousin. Instantly, her curiosity roused, Alex stood and walked towards the rocks, her eyes marking the vehicle's progress.

'Samuel, look . . . over there.'

Her brother was at first uncomprehending and then recognition dawned.

'It's that car,' he said. 'What's it doing there?'

A conspicuous sign on the farm gateway promised prosecution for trespassers. The farm and that car went together like ice cream and spinach.

'You know that car that was driving badly,' Alex said to her father as they drew close to the gently browning fish. 'Well, we just saw it driving over Manawaora Farm. Should it be there?'

'It's trespassing, Dad,' Samuel affirmed.

Greg took the tongs and turned the fish on the grill. Juice spattered on the glowing embers, sending up a small plume of steam.

'Could be,' he replied absently, reaching for his glass.

Alex looked at her brother and lifted an eyebrow. Dad was 'out of the office' when barbecuing.

Before long, he rose from his squatting position and stretched his back. Long-armed tongs dangled from his hand.

'It's ready,' he called. 'Come and get it.'

The fish was excellent—cooked to perfection. Greg served it from the grill straight on to their plates, and everyone helped themselves to the food that sprawled over a plastic beach table: a crunchy green salad garnished with sliced tomatoes, cucumber, and grated cheese; a jar of lustrous mayonnaise for the children and bottle of light Italian dressing for the adults; potato salad and baby beetroot; fresh bread and butter stacked on the bread wrapper and a bowl of salt-and-vinegar potato crisps. A bottle of white wine and a Tupperware jug of apple juice completed the spread.

They ate with the hunger that sea air inspires, Samuel pausing every now and again to throw stones in the direction of some seagulls hopeful of evening alms.

It was a sublime evening. Samuel raced to get the camera, at Fionna's request. Rich red clouds sucked the fire's glowing embers into a fading sky. As a computer screen saver, it would be a sweet reminder of summer on a bleak winter's day.

Conversation was heresy under the awesome canopy of changing light and colour. The sea eagerly offered its hues to the sky. The far shore pasted its silhouette upon a violet canvas.

The conductor swept his baton, and the cicada orchestra stopped abruptly.

Chapter 10

Motuarohia

The family sat at the breakfast table, their dirty plates stacked on the bench. Fionna and Greg were talking softly as each sipped a cup of tea, and Samuel was quietly urging Alex to make a bigger moustache than him with the Milo in her mug.

'So what would you kids like to do today?'

Both children were suddenly alert. Their smiling eyes locked, and together they shouted, 'Go to Roberton Island!'

Roberton Island was not immediately visible from their beach. Further around the rocks at the end of the point, it could be seen rising out of the sea, tantalisingly close, yet annoyingly too distant to reach except by motorboat or sail. A curious shark-fin hill thrust sharply upwards in the centre of its skyline. A shallow lagoon, flushed by each incoming tide, lay at its foot.

For many months, the sea thunders and explodes behind the wall of ancient rock that protects the lagoon from the open sea. At these times, urgent torrents surge through narrow crevices, depositing grey foam on the calmer water inside the lagoon. But in early summer, the ocean massages gently through those same inlets, its mirror surface blushed by the crimson blossom of pōhutukawa trees clinging grimly to the rock.

Every holiday they begged their father to take them on a day trip to the island. They found it infuriating that Dad often had excuses—reasons, he called them. There were so many different things to do at their own beach, yet Motuarohia, as it was named by Māori, offered adventures that were different from Clendon Point. That shark-fin hill had once been a Māori pā. The sheer rock face rising from the ocean swell was too steep to climb, and the very narrow pathway to the top fell away sharply on either side. It was easy to imagine how it had been fortified with walls of sharpened poles to hold off attacks from hostile tribes. There wasn't a great deal of space at the very top of the hill, but the views circled the compass.

Last year, Alex had sat up there with a keen warm wind tugging at her hair, when she had a strange experience. Watching yachts and launches bobbing their way towards Cape Brett, she suddenly grasped how God could see everything past, present, and future. Observing the passage of these boats, she knew where they had come from, where they were at that moment, and she could see where they were going—just like God. Well, nearly. She had found it hard to put this new understanding into words, so she had kept it to herself to ponder over. Alex was both excited and nervous about climbing that hill again. It had become a strangely spiritual place.

Samuel leaned enthusiastically over the table towards his father. 'Can we, Dad? Please, Dad!' They both searched their father's face for a signal. Dad briefly kept a straight face before a smile escaped his eyes.

'Yaaay!' Samuel yelled. 'Gee, thanks, Dad. That's what we've wanted most since we got here.' Instantly he was out of his chair.

'Really?' Greg responded in mock surprise. 'How come I didn't hear that before now?'

'Oh, Dad!' chided Alex.

'When can we go, Dad? Can we go real soon, like . . .' Samuel looked around the room. 'Like after we've done the dishes?'

'Hold on, boy.' Fionna had a few things to say. 'If we are going to spend more than thirty minutes there, we'll need something to eat and something to drink, won't we? While you two do the dishes, I'll get things together. You can both make your beds. And, Alex, you are responsible to see that you and Samuel get your hats, footwear, swimming things, and towels together. And remember the sunscreen,' she added as the two children raced to the kitchen sink.

Alex dropped over the stern of their runabout into the deliciously cool water and immediately adopted her slow, deliberate freestyle stroke. She was proud that her parents considered her old enough and skilled enough to be perfectly safe. Dad had instructed Samuel to stay on board so he could hold the boat at the water's edge when they reached the shore. He said he needed someone strong to do this while he and Mum unloaded everything. Samuel was not happy, and he immediately began to sulk.

Now Alex stood dripping at the water's edge, wiping salt water from her eyes. Dad had raised the outboard motor, and with token help from Samuel, he was energetically pushing the boat out from shore. As the boat lost way, he yanked on a light cord attached to the anchor perched on the bow, and with chain rattling over the side, it plunged to the sand below, securing the craft a good way out from shore. After two or three hours of receding tide, it would be close enough to shore to wade out to. If there was an emergency, he could haul on the cord and drag the anchor to shore with the boat in tow.

Alex and Samuel helped take the piled bags up the beach towards the line of driftwood and spiky grass.

'We'd better find some shade,' said Fionna. Then, indicating a pōhutukawa tree to the side of the lagoon, she led the way through coarse grass and low thorny bushes.

Rattling anchor chains announced the arrival of more boats seeking the shelter of the bay. Before long, small inflatables and dinghies would ferry their eager passengers to shore, all seeking shade from the sun. After a short absence, Samuel joined them, all signs of sulking gone.

'Alex, the lagoon's full. Let's go and explore,' he implored.

Alex was undecided. She had cooled down a lot from her swim to shore, and being dry now, she was not immediately keen to get wet again. 'I think I'll just watch you,' she said. Then seeing the disappointment on her brother's face she added, 'But later on, I'll come in and look at what you've found, OK?'

Satisfied, he sat down and hastily put the swim fins on his feet before flapping awkwardly through the coarse grass. Alex followed, choosing a sandy pathway through the grass and low spiky plants to the lagoon. She stood with her bare feet on the broken shells, warm water caressing her ankles. Samuel had already slid into the water, mask over his nose and eyes, snorkel at a jaunty angle, his head turning at every attraction on the lagoon bed.

Just beyond the rock barricade, Alex could hear pounding waves. She noted the slight swirling and swell of water funnelling through narrow passages into the lagoon. She inhaled the scents of sea air, hot sand, and sunburnt grass that reminded her so strongly of Bay of Islands' summers.

She gazed idly at Shark Fin Hill. Several figures, sharply silhouetted against a brilliant blue backdrop were making their way up the narrow path that led to the summit. One figure shorter than the others seemed to be pushing to get past. Eventually it succeeded and moved quickly to the top before disappearing from sight. She was about to shift her gaze when the figure reappeared and began performing strange arm and leg movements. Larger figures soon joined and began performing in unison. Then it dawned on Alex that they were performing a haka, a Māori war dance.

She watched with fascination. There on top of what was once a Māori fortification, some people were doing what might long ago have been performed to scare attackers off, or to build up the courage of those inside the pā. She imagined she could almost hear their fearsome voices and see their tattooed faces. The next moment, Samuel stood dripping in front of her.

'Come on, Alex, come and look at this. It's really cool.' She still didn't feel inclined, but she couldn't resist the excited look on her brother's face. Shortly, she joined him, complete with goggles, snorkel, and swim fins. Her reluctance soon dissolved in the tepid water. Each gentle kick of the fins propelled her to a new work of art on the constantly changing lagoon floor. Occasionally, Samuel loomed close by to gesture at something he wanted her to see.

After a while, the sandy bottom fell away, and she felt a cooler flow of water swelling through the wall of rock that separated ocean from lagoon. On the rock face ahead, a dark mass of seaweed swung and swayed with the tidal suck and swell. Scenes like this used to terrify her, but today she was just a little wary. She continued her slow approach, observing the pink sea skin that covered the rocks where sea snails and anemones pitted it like acne. Brown tentacles of kelp licked at her goggles at each inflow, then at the suck of the current, beckoned her eagerly to come and see what was hidden. Small iridescent fish shimmered in the middle of this action, almost motionless among the thrashing straps of kelp.

For a few minutes, Alex watched in fascination, only occasionally using her swim fins or arms to hold her position. Without warning, the fish darted in unison to make a new formation below the kelp. Alex drew a deep breath through her snorkel and dived gently after them.

Suddenly, her eyes widened and her heart pounded. As the current swept in and the kelp lifted, Alex saw the top of a human head wedged in a crevice, its strands of black hair drawn towards her as in an invisible wind. A white limb with swollen fingers rose momentarily on the current before disappearing behind the receding seaweed. At the very same moment, a shadow loomed nearby, and something grabbed her ankle firmly. Thrashing legs and arms wildly, she shot to the surface. Ripping the snorkel from her mouth, she gulped a choking mixture of salt water and air before a scream of terror rocketed from her mouth. Her fear-widened eyes searched the surface for the direction of the next attack. The next moment, Samuel's head burst through the surface, his hands already ripping off his goggles and snorkel.

'You didn't need to kick me in the face, Alex!' he yelled.

His face blazed red with anger as he also fought to gain his breath. 'You made my mouth bleed,' he added between coughing bouts. He inspected the diluted red water on the fingers he had just removed from his stinging face. His face crumpled, and he began to cry.

Ignoring his crying, Alex shouted, 'Samuel, don't you ever do that again! You nearly drowned me, you, you . . .' Several words came to mind, but they were words she did not use and her parents would certainly punish her for using them. Yet fear had pushed her too far, and if words would not do, there was always the other option. She slapped him on his nearest shoulder as hard as she could, and Samuel's strident wailing lifted several tones.

As relief surged through her, she could not stem her own flood of tears. The ghastly scene in the kelp had briefly been overshadowed by Samuel's scare, but now it came back to her as, first swimming then wading through the shallowing water, she made her way to the shore. Greg stood there, arms folded and a stern look on his face.

'What's going on out there between you two? Both of you crying,' he snorted. He looked severely at Alex, and as Samuel drew alongside, his wailings continuing in both pitch and volume, Dad turned his sternness onto him. 'Now, Samuel, stop it. Stop it right now!'

Mum's anxious face appeared. 'Here are your towels,' she offered. 'Get yourselves dried and—'

Alex took the towel. 'Dad, there's a dead body out in the water.' Seeing her father's uncomprehending face, she repeated, 'There's a dead body caught in the rocks and Samuel scared me when he grabbed my foot and I nearly drowned, so I hit him and I shouldn't have, but I was scared and I'm sorry.' Tears tumbled among the torrent of words, and she buried her head in the towel, her shoulders heaving as she crumpled to the sand.

Samuel's crying mysteriously ceased. 'Wow! You saw a dead person? What did it look like?' He crouched down beside her.

'Leave her alone, Samuel!' His mother's hand was firm on his shoulder. 'Now go up and get yourself properly dry and put a shirt on before you get burnt.' Samuel was about to protest but there was a no-nonsense tone in her voice, so he turned obediently towards their pōhutukawa tree, casting several looks back over his shoulder as he went.

Greg placed his arm around Alex's shaking shoulders. 'Slow down, girl. Tell me what you saw again.'

The gruesome image was etched black and white in her mind. She shuddered and took a slow breath before saying, 'Dad, there was someone's head stuck in the rock under the seaweed, and I was only this far away.' She drew her arms apart almost full length. Then seeing the disbelief on her father's face, she continued more emphatically. 'I saw the top of its head. It had black hair. There really is someone down there, Dad,' she implored.

'It's easy to imagine things under the water. It could have been a clump of seaweed with strands that look like hair. How could a body get in there, do you think?' The detective used reasoning. Alex used feelings, feelings that were well roused at that moment.

'I don't know,' she sang in exasperation. 'Just go and have a look for yourself if you don't believe me!'

She noted her father's widening eyes and, for a moment, regretted speaking to him in that manner. He stood up, and there was a moment's silence before he spoke. 'OK. I think maybe I'd better. Detectives need to check out all stories, don't they?'

Alex got to her feet. 'I'm not making it up. It really is there. Thank you, Dad,' she added softly.

She meekly followed her father to where Mum was kneeling in the shade of the pōhutukawa tree, talking earnestly to Samuel, who was trying to look everywhere but at her face. She just had time to overhear her saying, 'Imagine if it was you—' before she broke off, seeing the two approaching figures.

'I'm going to have a look.' Greg spoke in an even tone as he reached in his beach bag for his goggles. 'Well, it won't hurt, will it?' he responded as Fionna looked inquiringly at him.

'Can I come?' Samuel pleaded.

'Sure,' said Greg.

'Greg!'

'What?'

Fionna looked flushed. 'You're not really going to take him, are you?'

'Yep. He deserves to see this. I think it would be a very good lesson for him.'

Alex was puzzled about the wink her father sent her. And then, despite

Fionna's protestations, he instructed Samuel to grab his diving things. In an instant, Samuel was struggling to get the fins over his sandy feet. Then scrabbling under his towel for his goggles and snorkel, and turning a deaf ear to his mother's advice, he flapped like a duck after his father.

Greg turned. 'Come and tell me where to look, Alex,' he called.

She stood alongside him and pointed out the features of the rocky outcrop across the curve of the lagoon. 'Actually, it would be quicker to walk around and get in the water there.'

She pointed to the sandy strip that formed an arc below the lower slopes of Shark Fin Hill. Observing the approval in her father's face, she led off, each step more confident.

Samuel protested as he fell further behind. His goggles were over his eyes, snorkel attached, and his feet flapped ridiculously as the fins threatened to trip him. Finally, sense prevailed and he removed his fins, then carrying one in each hand, he caught up to them. The snorkel still wiggled perilously from the attachment to his goggles.

'What a clown!' Alex offered. Her brother responded with facial expressions and exaggerated movements. He quite liked the description. Soon, Alex slowed then stopped in the last spot of sun before a shadow darkened the water and rock.

'See where there's that big crack.' She pointed precisely, making sure her father identified the exact spot. 'Well, that's one of the places the water gets through, and down under, there's a lot of seaweed where the water makes a current.' She paused and drew in a deep breath. 'You dive below it and . . .' Her voice trailed off. She looked up at her father's tanned face. He smiled curiously. He washed his goggles in the lagoon water before fitting them precisely and tightening the rubber straps.

'Come on, Samuel,' he called. 'Let's do some body surfing . . . er, searching.'

Alex watched them lunge through the water until it was deep enough to dive forward. Then she walked back to sit on the grass above the sand, watching their progress with clashing emotions. She wanted desperately to be proved right. At the same time, she was scared about a body being there. She knew there was a body. She had seen it with her own eyes. Clearly. She sensed that her father didn't really believe there was a body.

'What are you doing here?'

Alex squeaked involuntarily. 'Oh, man!' she yelped. Her chest rose and fell rapidly as she clapped her hands to her mouth, turning her whole body at the voice. 'You frightened the living daylights out of me, Hāmuera!' Her breathing became more normal, but her face glowed red. 'What are *you* doing here?'

'I asked you first.' White teeth erupted from the cheeky smile that framed his glinting eyes. 'So what are *you* doing here?' he repeated.

Did she tell him everything only to have Dad say she had been dreaming, there was nothing there? *Better to close your mouth and be thought a fool than to open your mouth and prove it beyond all doubt*, her father often quoted. It made real sense to her now.

'Oh, just having a day on the island. We always come here at least once each holidays. It's my very favourite island. We have such fun, and it doesn't usually matter what the weather is like. It's a kind of mysterious island, and there's this lagoon and Shark Fin Hill up there and good swimming.' She became aware that she was talking rather fast. 'OK, so what are *you* doing here?'

'We come here every year too. We come to invoke the spirit of our ancestor.'

Noting the change in the girl's face, he carried on in conspiratorial tones. 'One night, not far from this very spot in fact, my ancestor, Wiremu Maketu, smashed a pākehā man's skull with an axe. The next day, he killed a pākehā woman and three kids who lived in the same house.'

'But why?'

'The man treated him pretty stink. He wouldn't pay him for the work he did. The man kicked him, and that offended Wiremu's mana. The lady swore at him. She shouldn't have done that, 'cause it made it worse.'

'How long ago was this?' A vision of the underwater body momentarily flashed into her head.

'A long time ago, back when pākehā began to take over our land. Anyway, he was really mad at them. They say there was so much blood all over the place and their bodies were so cut up, he must have been pretty much out of his mind.'

'But that's horrible. I mean, the children weren't responsible.' She looked appalled.

Hāmuera continued, 'Wiremu ran home for protection from utu because one of the children he killed was a granddaughter of a chief from a different tribe.'

'What's utu?'

'Revenge.'

'So what happened to him?'

'After some kōrerō, his father gave him to the British soldiers. He didn't want to start a war with the other tribe.' He paused and looked down before continuing in a low voice. 'He was the first person to be hung for murder in New Zealand. It took far longer than a quick blow with a mere. Māori men who saw the punishment thought it was a shocking way to die.' A distant look came across his face.

They sat silently side by side, idly pulling at blades of grass. Suddenly, both heads jerked around as a high-pitched shriek echoed across the lagoon. Samuel's voice was heard over the water. 'Dad! Don't do that! You frightened the living daylights out of me.'

There was a moment of splashing mixed with Greg's indistinct words and his laugh. Alex caught the baffled look on the Māori boy's face.

'Don't worry. That's Samuel with my dad. I think Dad just taught him a lesson.' She smiled a smug smile. She guessed Samuel now knew what *he* had done to *her* was like. It served him right.

After a short silence, Hāmuera continued in a low voice. 'He's still pretty mad about it, you know.'

'Who?'

'Wiremu. His spirit is here and he still wants to get even. Ever since he was hanged, at least one person connected with the island dies each year that no karakia is said.'

'Karakia? What's that?'

'Prayers. Special words that speak to our ancestors. Karakia tell them that the living are keeping their memory and their honour alive. If they have been dishonoured in their death, then they seek revenge from the spirit world.'

Alex hid her growing alarm. 'You don't really believe all that, do you? About someone having to die each year unless you do your prayer thing?'

'My aunty believes it. She says we are too late this year. The cicadas didn't sing before Christmas. Someone's already been killed.'

Alex wanted to say something, but the words wouldn't form properly in her head. Hāmuera had nothing more to say and so the two sat silently, side by side. The dull pounding of the sea and muted sounds of children playing barely registered above their individual thoughts.

She was unsure how long she had been lost in thought when her brain became instantly alert. Her father was wading through the shallow water in her direction, Samuel gliding slowly behind, his snorkel erect, still searching for lagoon treasures. Alex met her father as he splashed the last few metres, searching his face for any clues.

He was about to speak when his eyes refocussed behind her. 'What's that Māori boy doing here?'

'That's Hāmuera, Dad.'

'I know who he is. I thought your mother and I said not to knock around with him.'

'I'm not knocking around with him. I didn't even know he was here. He found me here, and we were just talking.' Alex sounded defensive.

Greg strode off, ignoring Hāmuera as he passed. Then calling over his shoulder, he ordered, 'You'd better come with me. Now,' he added.

She glanced at Hāmuera and shrugged. 'I've got to go now. See you around,' she said. Hāmuera gave a quick upward nod, and his smile was brief.

As she turned, quick reflexes stopped her from falling over Samuel removing his fins on the sand just behind her. 'Watch out,' she said edgily, and followed the large imprints of her father's feet in the sand.

Her brother got to his feet and, after a brief word to Hāmuera, trotted after her, the snorkel still attached to his goggles bouncing awkwardly, and a fin in each hand,

Greg had reached their picnic spot and was talking to Fionna when Alex threaded her way through the grass from the lagoon. He reached in his beach bag just as she arrived and drew out his cell phone.

'You were right.' he said simply. He pressed some keys in rapid succession. 'There's a body all right.'

He placed the phone to his ear. 'Yes, hello, sergeant. Greg Armstrong, Auckland Central, here again. I'm afraid your boys have another job today. There's a body in the lagoon on Roberton Island. Any reports of a recent missing person?' He listened for a moment.

'OK, so I'll keep the area as a crime scene until you bring the stuff. No, it's actually submerged. Probably a good idea to bring some scuba gear.'

Alex didn't listen to the rest of the call. There really was a body. Her skin pricked with goose bumps. Hāmuera's aunty had said the prayer thing had been too late this year. Someone had already been killed. And she, Alex, had found the body.

A gust of wind bent the grass as the sun slid behind a cloud. A single cicada began its rasping in a bough above her. Almost immediately, there was a noisy flurry of insect and bird wings and then, silence.

Chapter 11

Manawaora

Greg looked serious. After his early morning climb up the track to telephone the Russell police station, Alex was eager for information.

'What did they say, Dad?' Alex prompted.

He hesitated before answering. 'Well, it looks like it was someone off a foreign fishing vessel, most likely Korean. Definitely Asian.'

'The poor fellow,' Fionna said. 'Coming all this way and then drowning so far from home. How dreadful for his family.'

Greg hesitated again. 'They don't think he drowned.'

There was silence while everyone considered the options. Alex fought the shiver forming between her shoulder blades.

'What happened, then?' she asked.

'They can't be sure until the pathologist reports back, but they think he was deliberately killed.'

'Did he have a knife in his back, or was his throat cut or something?' Samuel probed, keen to learn any gory details.

'There were signs of injury consistent with serious assault,' Greg replied, hoping a formal explanation would satisfy. It was a forlorn hope.

'So he was really bashed up. Was he tortured too?' Without waiting for an answer, he began rehearsing a few scenarios complete with actions. 'He could have done something he shouldn't have, or he knew a secret and they tried to get it out of him. Or maybe there was a fight on the boat. Yeah, everyone was against him and he got badly hurt, but he knocked out some of them, 'cause he's such a good kung fu fighter, but there were too many of them so he dived overboard and he drowned.'

'Yep. I reckon that just about covers it.' Greg smiled and looked across at Fionna. 'So what's for breakfast?'

'I don't know. It's your turn.'

'I'll make it,' Alex offered. 'What about scrambled eggs and fried tomatoes?'

Greg looked grateful. 'Thanks, Princess. I have a couple of things I really must do that shouldn't take too long, so that would be great if you don't mind. All right with you, Mum?'

Fionna smiled, Greg left, Samuel continued building a *Star Wars* model, and Alex busied herself toasting bread, frying tomatoes, and scrambling eggs. Fionna watched with guarded pride from a distance.

With encouragement from Samuel, who was ravenous, Alex was taking steaming plates to the table when Greg returned.

'That looks excellent. Hasn't she done well?' he said, and with a quick thank you to Alex, and God, they began eating.

'What I don't understand', said Alex as Greg cleared the table later, 'is how that body got to where it did. Those overseas fishing boats aren't allowed to come in close, are they?'

'If they have a licence from the government, they can fish inside our three hundred and seventy kilometres zone, but it's illegal to fish inside about twenty from shore, so basically you're right.'

'Did the police say how long he had been in the water?'

'Three days maybe. They can tell by the condition of the skin.' In anticipation of the question forming on Samuel's lips, he added, 'And no, I don't know what it looks like, so don't ask.'

Samuel returned to playing *Star Wars.*

'So his boat must have been in quite close to the bay, probably even closer than twenty kilometres, which means it probably happened at night,' Alex mused.

'Because?' Greg inquired.

'Because it would take longer than three days for his body to get to the island if they were way out at sea, wouldn't it?' Her father nodded. 'And the boat would attract attention in daylight if it was close in. I don't think they would want that.'

'But why would they come in close to drop a body over the side if there was a good chance of it being found?'

'Dad,' she drawled. 'They didn't come in close to drop the body overboard. There was another reason for that.'

'Which was?'

Alex looked bemused. 'I don't know, do I? You're the detective.'

Greg grinned. 'You've been doing a very good job of it so far. Well done, my girl. Good thinking, but we can only guess the reason at the moment.'

'I know,' Samuel's voice intruded. 'They came to get some marigana.' Neither father nor sister corrected him as they considered his suggestion.

'Well, I guess that's as good a reason as any. You might just be right, Samuel,' Greg responded, his eyebrows arched in the 'well, how about that?' position.

'Thanks, Dad,' he said, without looking up from his play.

It was a possibility, and the thought that the marijuana from Clendon Point could be linked to a murder at sea made Alex's heart race.

'Hey, everybody, we've got things to do and places to go. No more scary talk, OK? Gran and Grandpa will be here tomorrow, so let's make sure everything is nice for them.' Fionna moved to the bench and began to heat the water in readiness for washing the dishes. Greg joined her.

Alex slid onto her bunk and watched her brother's nimble fingers rearrange plastic toy parts into a customised pirate space ship. He seemed immersed in his designing, so Alex was slightly startled when he said, 'It probably was drugs. Hāmuera's cousin is a gang sort of person. I bet he knows something.'

Alex was silent for a while. Disconnected thoughts and vague impressions began to assemble like a magnet attracting iron filings.

'Would you like to come for a row later, Samuel?'

'You want to go fishing?' Her brother looked up, instantly alert.

'Not this time.' She leaned closer in and spoke quietly. 'I think we need to check out something at the farm.' She glanced towards her parents before holding an index finger to her lips to silence any further questions. She mouthed the word 'marijuana'.

His concentration now completely broken, Samuel began stuffing spare parts into a plastic bag. He placed the futuristic space vessel on his pillow, and with a feigned air of innocence, he interrupted his parents to ask if there was something they could do to help. As usual, Mum had a mental list of things that needed to be done. Dad was going to make a trip into Russell, so the rubbish needed to be bagged then taken up to the station wagon for him to drop off at the tip. Fuel tanks and a gas bottle that needed refilling could go up also. The house needed to be vacuum-cleaned and aired and the outdoor furniture put out on the deck. Brother and sister divided the tasks that could be done separately and agreed to work on preparing the house together. There was not the usual debate over why, nor who should do it.

By mid-morning, all tasks were completed. Mum checked over the house, and she was very pleased with what they had done. She was going to organise a few other things in the house and wait there until Dad returned.

Dad, softened by their willing helpfulness, gave permission for them to take the dinghy for a row as long as they kept their life jackets on. As they hurried down the track, Alex took the opportunity to elaborate her thoughts to Samuel.

'Remember the other night when we had the barbecue on the beach and we saw that car over on the farm? Well, we wondered what it was doing there, right?'

Samuel remembered.

'Now change the question,' she continued. 'Let me ask you, where was the car coming from?'

Samuel looked puzzled. 'It was going along a track back to the road.'

'Yes, Samuel. I know where it was going, but where had it come from when we saw it? If we can work out where it was coming from, we might know why it was there in the first place.'

They grabbed their life jackets from the bach and hurried down to the beach. The tide had receded, leaving a wide expanse of sand and pebbles.

'Come on,' she said. 'Go to those rocks where we saw the car from the other night, then you might get the same answer as me.'

They jogged in silence, but before they had reached the spot, Samuel exclaimed, 'I know. That barn or boat shed or whatever it is!'

'Exactly,' said Alex, breathing quickly as they came to a halt in full view of Manawaora Farm.

They stood alongside each other, gazing across the water at the wide stretch of shoreline from which folds of green and straw-yellow fields rose towards a distant line of bush. At the extreme end of the beach, at the foot of a steeply rising hill and enfolded by a cluster of trees, they observed the corrugated iron building.

'Where else could it have come from.' It was less a question than a statement.

'So that's where we're going, aren't we?' Samuel said, with a tremor of excitement. 'Come on, let's go.'

Quickly retracing their steps along the beach, they untied the dinghy, each of them trying to take over from the other's fumbling fingers. As they put on their life jackets, they debated over who should row the dinghy. But by the time they dragged it to the water and the oars were secured in their rollicks, they had agreed that Samuel could row first, and at halfway, if he wasn't tired before then, Alex would take over.

Clendon Cove was sheltered, but once clear of the point, a stiff north-westerly breeze across the beam pushed them towards the wrong end of Manawaora Bay. Alex encouraged Samuel to pull harder on the right oar and keep the bow pointing at the opposite shore. He concentrated grimly, but before they had reached halfway, he was happy to accept his sister's offer to swap places. He sat in the stern, red-faced and breathing heavily, the effort having temporarily drained his energy.

Alex settled into a rhythm that moved them steadily closer to the scrub-covered hills of the far shore despite the choppy sea. Occasionally, a raised blade threatened to pull out of her grasp as its tip caught in a swell. Meanwhile, Samuel took the plastic bailer Dad had fashioned from a two-litre milk container and began busily bailing water from a deepening pool that slopped around their feet.

Just when her muscles began to beg for rest, Alex heard the approaching rasp of cicadas in the mānuka scrub that straggled up the slopes behind her. Now that they were close enough, she began to follow the shoreline, the breeze and waves carrying them towards the beach, occasional oar pulls sufficient to keep them on course.

Holding the oars clear of the water, she turned in her seat to take in the nearing building. A wide concrete ramp led up from the beach to large double doors. The tall side wall was topped by a rounded roof in which translucent panels were set to compensate for the lack of windows. Apart from these panels, everything was bush-green-painted corrugated iron. If it wasn't for its large dimensions, it could have been a boat shed. If it wasn't for the ramp down to the water, it could have been a barn.

Alex nodded over her shoulder in the direction of the building. 'I don't think we should go right to the ramp. That would make it obvious they have visitors. See if there's somewhere just ahead where we can get in among the rocks.'

Samuel spotted a miniature beach, which Alex agreed would be perfect. Rocks provided a screen from the farm, and calm water led to a small slope of sand. She navigated the narrow gap in the rocks, and with several gentle pulls on the oars, the dinghy ghosted forward and nudged the sand. Samuel clambered out while Alex stowed the oars, then together they hauled the dinghy as far above the tide line as they could. There was no fun in returning to find the boat floating far out from the shore.

Without wind and wave noises, the mānuka scrub vibrated with cicada song. Alex felt a surge of excitement as she removed her life jacket. This was turning into the sort of adventure she might read about; only this time, she was an actual character in a real-life murder-and-drugs mystery.

Samuel began climbing gingerly up the rocks, and Alex noted how brightly the yellow jacket and red cords stood out—wonderful for detection and rescue from the water, but an absolute giveaway if trespassing. As she urgently called him back, she accepted they would, in fact, be trespassing the moment they strayed above the high-water mark.

Following his sister's example, Samuel wedged his jacket between the transom and back seat of the dinghy. He was fidgeting with excitement, and Alex realised he was unaware of the potential danger they faced if discovered, especially if criminals were doing criminal things.

'Samuel, listen,' she said intensely. 'If there are bad people around here, then bad things could happen to us if they find us, so you must do as I say and try not to be seen. Have you got that?' He nodded.

'OK, now keep your eyes wide open, and if you see anybody, duck down or find a place to hide.'

Apprehension chased excitement from her brother's face. 'Have you seen someone?'

'No, but that doesn't mean there's nobody about. And even if they're not here now, someone could arrive at any time, so just be careful. If we get separated for any reason, we meet back at the dinghy. We wait for each other, OK?'

They moved off, and Alex stifled a giggle as Samuel adopted covert movements more suited to a spy movie, ducking low and dashing from shelter to cover after careful surveillance.

Footwear was one thing Alex had not thought about. Their feet were not yet toughened by a barefoot summer. They carefully picked their way over sea-smoothed rocks and through the mānuka scrub. She was relieved when they arrived at a grass strip that separated the large building from the trees they were wending through. Halting among the sooty, thin tree trunks, they cautiously surveyed the scene.

It was an imposing construction for a farm building, and she noted that across the front doors, a strong wooden beam was set horizontally in metal brackets and secured by brass padlocks at each end. Heat shimmered off the impenetrable side wall, which appeared even longer close up. The rear of the building, partly shaded by several tall poplars and a sprawling pōhutukawa tree, offered cover if they needed to remain hidden. Hopefully, that wouldn't be needed.

Samuel's voice sounded suddenly loud. 'So what are we looking for, then?'

He looked up at his sister, and she observed indecision in his eyes. There was a fast pulsing on the side of his throat as he licked dry lips.

'There could be drugs, like you thought this morning. There might be nothing. Let's just look, be detectives, OK?'

He waited for further instructions. The easy part was over. Alex hadn't formulated a plan for this part of the adventure. She had to think quickly.

'Well, it doesn't look too hopeful at the front. It's all padlocked, but let's have a closer look anyway. You never know.'

An inspection confirmed her fears. It was well and truly secured, and the gap below the iron cladding was so small they could only get a slight glimpse of what lay inside when they put their faces to the ground.

'Looks like a lot of hay,' Alex said.

'I think there's a boat too, over that side, and wheels. It could be a boat trailer,' Samuel suggested.

'We need to see if there's some other way in. You go around that side, and I'll go around this way. I'll meet you round the back,' Alex instructed. 'And be careful.'

Samuel peered cautiously around the corner of the building before disappearing. Alex took a last look at the doors and, satisfied there was no possibility of entry at the front, set off on her own stealthy inspection.

It was just as she had thought. The continuous iron sheeting was unbroken by anything resembling door or window down her side. She reached the shaded rear at the same instant as Samuel, who, with a shrug of his shoulders, indicated the same for his side.

Almost immediately, their eyes settled on a large door set in the back wall. It was narrower than those at the front and not as tall. As they approached, Alex noted wheel tracks in recently flattened grass. And although the door was secured with a strong bolt and padlock, there was a greater gap below the iron. They automatically knelt and, with their faces to the ground, peered into the interior.

'It's too dark. The trees don't let enough light in through the roof panels,' Alex exclaimed in disappointment. 'I can't see anything, can you, Samuel?' Samuel didn't reply.

'Samuel?' she repeated.

She looked up. Her brother's head and shoulders were pushed under the iron. His body writhed eel-like. His feet blindly searched for grip to push him forward. Amid grunts and gasps, his muffled voice replied, 'I can get in, Alex. Push on my feet.'

Without hesitation, she positioned herself behind him and began pushing his feet with her hands, but each time he pressed against them, she fell backward. After several experiments, she found that by standing with her feet sideways immediately behind his, he could push against them and get sufficient forward movement to inch ahead. Soon, much of his body had passed under the door. Only his bottom and legs remained.

'I'm stuck, Alex, I'm stuck. Help me!' There was panic in Samuel's voice. The material of his trousers was bunched and caught on the sharp edge of the corrugated iron.

'Samuel, your pants are the problem. They're caught up.'

'I'm not taking them off.' His muffled voice came in heightened tones.

'You don't need to, silly,' Alex said through a broad grin. 'Put your hand back and pull on them. I'll help from this side.'

It was evident from his grunting that lying prone under a narrow gap made it difficult to get a hand to his belt, but eventually, she detected the material moving and the bunches begin to smooth. She pressed on his buttocks and trousers to assist, but this evoked an immediate protest. Even in dire circumstances, his modesty prevailed. After further wriggling and grunting, the trousers disappeared, followed quickly by his legs.

'What can you see?' Alex questioned.

'Give me a chance. Let me have a look around first. It's pretty big.' His voice sounded more distant as he spoke.

Alex stood looking sightlessly at the door. Her gaze shifted thoughtfully from the door to the gap under which her brother had wriggled and back again. She pictured all sorts of possibilities as the cacophony of cicadas pervaded the silence. Sun-scorched mānuka scented the air. A blowfly thrummed past and settled briefly to preen its wings on the wall. The world slowed.

She had lost track of time when the sound interrupted her thoughts. For an instant, she felt dislocated, like waking from a dream. It took a moment to register the sound of an approaching truck engine. It was in a low gear and coming towards them.

'Samuel' she called urgently. 'Someone's coming!'

Chapter 12

The Asian

It wasn't as dark inside as it had appeared, looking under the door. Samuel could see the side walls quite clearly in the dim light. Two slender metal girders stretched from wall to wall, spaced evenly between the translucent roof panels above. A single electric light cable hung from the centre of each, with an unshielded light bulb hung at their ends.

To the left of the furthest girder, a large frame was suspended with ropes attached to each corner, and to the right, a faint outline of what appeared to be a flat-roofed room projected some five metres from a shadowy dividing wall. A concrete strip wide enough for two cars stretched from the doorway towards the wall. On either side, bare ground spread to the sides. There was a lot of unused space—not a lot to get excited about.

While that was disappointing, Samuel felt nervous excitement at the thought of being caught trespassing. He began a quick inspection. At least he could then report everything to his sister—like a good spy reporting to his spymaster.

A solid post cemented into the ground near the wall held the frame aloft through a simple rope-and-pulley system. A single rope was secured in figures of eight around a holder fixed on to its side. There seemed no logical reason for the arrangement, and this intrigued him. From beneath, the contents looked dark but not dense. He took hold of the rope to test the weight. It gave a little, so he guessed that whatever was up there was not all that heavy.

Curiosity won over caution. Unwinding the rope with his left hand, he took the strain with the other. He began to feel the weight pull on his right hand as the last windings slipped. Quickly grasping the rope in both hands, he took the strain and was relieved to discover the pulleys made the lowering task manageable.

At eye level, he intuitively recognised the drying plant material. No wonder the search for a launch had proved fruitless. The marijuana, spread out in wilting bundles over chicken netting, was several layers high.

At that very moment, the sound of an approaching vehicle rumbled the corrugated iron wall. Almost instantly, his sister's urgent voice called, 'Samuel, someone's coming!'

He let the frame fall to the ground and began to run back to the doorway. He froze as he assessed the impossibility of squeezing under the door and escaping in time. His eyes searched feverishly for somewhere to hide. For one moment, he thought of standing where the door would swing back against the wall and hide him. What if they closed the door after them? He would be exposed like a crab under an overturned rock. Instead he scuttled to the far corner of the internal back wall, as far away as possible from the doorway. But now he figured that even there, a flood of light could expose him when the door opened.

In the dimness, his eyes locked on to a previously invisible door frame set into the back wall. With a flood of relief, he ran to it and wrenched the door handle. It turned but wouldn't open. He turned it the other way. No matter which way the handle turned or how much he cannoned his shoulder against the door, his increasingly frenzied efforts had no effect.

Everything froze. His widened eyes followed the sound of an engine passing outside. His ears pictured a truck rounding the building and stopping outside the rear door. The engine idled. A door slammed.

He fought the panic threatening to overtake him. His eyes darted like reflections off the late afternoon sea. There was nowhere to hide. Discovery was imminent.

And then he saw it, a slim chance. The timber framing of the internal wall provided a crude ladder to the flat roof of the room. He could lie upon the roof.

Without further thought, he sprinted to where room and wall joined and began to climb. There was little depth between the corrugated iron and timber framing for hands or feet. His knees pressed into the iron and threatened to loosen his hand grip. Automatically he twisted his body and feet sideways. It became easier to reach up and continue the climb.

Above his laboured panting, he heard the sound of men's voices. At the same time, a clattering on iron let him know the padlock on the outside door was being unlocked. The bolt slid across its holders, and a small chink of light slipped across the floor.

His right hand patted the roof of the room, and he thrust blindly upwards for the wood above his other hand. For one terrifying moment, his fingers seemed unable to hold his weight. He pressed his body closer to the wall, muscles trembling with nervous exertion before finding a new holding for one foot. This relieved the weight, and in desperation, he renewed his hand grip.

The door began to open, and in that instant, he dived to place his other hand on the flat roof as well, immediately pushing off the wall with his legs. All his weight rested on arms and shoulders as, poised with head straining forward over the flat roof, he fought for balance.

And then, unable to take the weight any more, his arms gave way. Face and torso fell to the dust-encrusted roof. Legs flailed in the air, and hands grappled forward for a handhold. The roof, smooth and treacherous with accumulated dust, offered no grip. He felt himself slowly sinking back over the edge.

Just as the door swung wide, streaming light across the floor, his left leg kicked against the wall. With renewed energy, he positioned his body so his toes gained a solid foothold and summoned all his strength. The next moment, he was crabbing on elbows and knees over the flat surface.

The engine revved and the gear box clunked. The driver drove forward a small distance before noisily engaging reverse gear. Samuel watched warily from his sanctuary as the truck backed through the doorway, closing out the light as it came. Its exhaust beat an increasingly loud tattoo against the walls, and the distinctive aroma of diesel fumes tickled his nostrils. A voice shouted, then the motor stopped.

'You could have come back further, but no matter, Sid. She's right,' a rural Kiwi accent twanged. The cab door opened, and Sid stepped down. He walked a little gingerly to the rear of the truck, leaving his door ajar.

'Yeah. I guess I could',' he said, assessing the distance between vehicle and room. Samuel instinctively pressed himself flat on the roof.

Sid wore tight denim work shorts that ended halfway up his solid thighs. A stained yellow T-shirt stretched tightly over his protruding stomach. Brown leather work boots with grey woollen socks slumped around his ankles. He was a short man, and as he stretched his arms above his head and bent forward to flex his back, thin strands of hair flopped forward, revealing a large bald patch. 'Man, I'm stiff. Only twice out of my seat and what have we done, about five hundred kays, do ya think, Colin?'

''Bout that, but we had to get as far as possible by night. No need to draw unnecessary attention, eh.'

Sid practised some knee bends. 'Guess we can't get unloaded before the others arrive. Our Mr Liu will want to check the cargo for sure before we put it away. Did they say how long it will be before it's moved out?'

'Nah. They only tell how much they need and when it needs to be here by and when we get paid for the delivery. I bet they make a packet.'

That seemed to remind him of something, and he returned to the cab. Reaching across to the passenger side, he retrieved a pack of cigarettes. 'Want one?' he said, offering the opened pack to Sid.

'Nah. Rather have one of them joints right now. Relax me a bit, you know, mellow out.' He laughed.

Colin tapped a cigarette on the pack before pulling a lighter out of his pocket. The lighter flashed, and the cigarette glowed as he drew a mouthful of smoke deeply into his lungs. He tilted his head back and blew the smoke into the air.

'Here they come,' Colin announced as he walked towards the door. Samuel lifted his head at the sound of another approaching vehicle and observed Colin's lean body framed in the doorway.

Samuel recognised the car that pulled up outside. The engine stopped, and the driver prised himself from behind the steering wheel.

Samuel did not recognise the man who slammed the passenger door, but something about the way he moved and held himself as he joined the driver suggested this man was dangerous. He stood one head taller than Hāmuera's cousin. His black T-shirt accentuated well-defined shoulder and chest muscles and seemed barely able to contain the huge biceps that forced his arms into brackets at each side. From a distance, his eyes were dark holes among the tousle of hair that merged with his beard.

Piri made the introductions. 'This here's my colleague Mākutu. Mākutu, this here's Colin, and back there is Sid, the driver.'

The stick figure and ogre shook hands.

'Weren't expecting you. Thought you were our Mr Liu, Piri.'

'Come to check how the drying's going,' Piri explained. 'Harvesting it early, there's a lot more moisture, and it takes longer to dry. Gotta be careful it doesn't rot, eh.'

'Sure. Go ahead,' Colin responded. His tone rippled with submission before, in a weak attempt to regain some authority, he added, 'Probably not a good idea to be here when Mr Liu arrives though.'

He stood aside as Mākutu moved towards the central wall. Colin waited for Piri then followed hesitantly at a distance.

'Hey, what the . . . What's going on here?' Piri's confusion and anger penetrated each syllable. 'Why's the stuff on the ground? What are you two . . .' He paused briefly enough for his anger to transform into rage. 'You're trying to rip us off, you . . .' His language rapidly deteriorated amid accusation and curses.

Mākutu cut off Sid's move to the truck cab, moving smoothly for a man of his size and, in a single motion, reached in to remove the ignition keys. Sid held his palms up at shoulder level in a gesture of surrender as the ogre dangled the keys tauntingly before him.

'We haven't done nothing,' Colin protested in a quavering voice. 'Honest, Piri. We didn't even know you had stuff on the rack yet. It was like that when we got here. Well, it must have been, because we didn't even notice it. We only just arrived. I didn't even have time to finish me fag.' He held the half-smoked cigarette out as proof.

Piri paused to assess the situation. The marijuana was intact. He inspected the rope and pulleys quickly. They were intact. He stared for a moment at the doorway.

'Was the door locked when you got here?' he asked.

The stick figure nodded assurance. The distant rasping of cicadas drifted through the open door. Time stood still. Samuel's breath came rapid and shallow. Piri began slowly hauling the rope through the pulleys until it became taut.

'If you ever double-cross us, you're dead meat, bro.' Mākutu's high-pitched voice might have raised a smile coming from such a big man in other circumstances. No one smiled. He tossed the keys at Sid and ambled over to the frame, where he rotated the position of several bundles of marijuana, examining their condition as he did so. With the faintest of nods, he showed his approval and gestured for the frame to be raised.

'If it slipped before, it won't this time,' Piri said as the frame reached its raised position. He wrapped the rope in careful figures of eight before tying off with three half hitches and pulling sharply on the tail several times.

'Stop there!' Samuel jumped with alarm at the unexpected voice. The Asian accent was unmistakable. The clipped tones added to the menace of the pistol extended in his left hand.

'Who you? What you doing here?' He motioned with his pistol at the two men by the rope.

'It's OK, Mr Liu. They share the shed,' Colin said. 'There's been a little misunderstanding, but we've sorted it out now.'

The pistol lowered. An awkward silence followed, and no one moved. Finally, Mākutu walked slowly towards Mr Liu, his right hand held out.

'Gidday, Mr Liu. Pleased to meet you.'

The pistol levelled again. 'Please, no come. You leave now. Goodbye.' He motioned with his pistol in an arc that reached the doorway.

Mākutu shrugged. 'No probs, bro. No sweat.'

Piri shuffled in his wake to the doorway. As they reached the car, he diverted to the back of the car, raised the boot, and slammed it shut before easing into the driver's seat. The car sank appreciably on its suspension. Mākutu paused on the other side and took a long look through the doorway, where Mr Liu stood motionless with the pistol still in his hand.

He pressed into the passenger seat. The car sank further. His door slammed. The motor revved rebelliously, and as the car lurched forward, a raised finger gestured from the open front passenger's window.

Chapter 13

Captured

The vehicle was approaching rapidly, and when Samuel didn't respond to her urgent call, Alex realised she must find cover—immediately. Panic blurred her vision as she frantically searched. Finally, the throb of the slowing engine forced a decision.

The next moment she was grappling the rough bark of the pōhutukawa tree, desperately stretching for higher boughs even as the truck rounded the corner of the building and came to a halt in front of the door.

From her perch, Alex watched a black, peaked cap jump down from the passenger side and walk purposefully towards the corrugated iron door. As an afterthought, it turned and came back to the driver's door, where it paused momentarily before returning, swinging a set of keys. Alex stared in horrified fascination as the unlocked bolt slid to the side and a light strip appeared then widened as the door disappeared inside.

The vehicle clunked into gear and drove forward, stopping directly beneath her tree. The windowless rear section was separated from the cab. If she had wanted, she could have lowered herself onto its roof like the heroic characters in books and movies, but Alex did not feel remotely heroic.

The driver noisily selected reverse gear before backing through the gaping doorway. She heard a faint shout, and her first thought was that Samuel had been discovered.

Please, God, don't let him be caught. Please. Run, Samuel!

The motor stopped. Her ears became her sole sense. The faint voices seemed to be in conversation. Gradually, she released her tense grip on the branch.

Thank you, God. Thank you so much.

Samuel must have found somewhere to hide.

As she raised herself from a crouched position, cruel pins and needles surged through her legs. She didn't dare move until the strength returned to her weakened knees. Meanwhile, she searched for a higher perch on which to sit rather than crouch.

She was about to relocate when she heard the approaching rumble of another motor. She was deciding whether to risk further pins and needles and crouch again or to keep standing, when a car swung around the corner of the building and stopped across the open doorway.

Despite her elevated position, she recognised the car. Hāmuera's cousin emerged from the driver's side. A huge man unfolded from the other side and walked around to join him. They stood together, looking into the building.

The thin man, wearing his black cap, stepped from the shadowy interior. Hāmuera's cousin greeted him and introduced his companion. They shook hands. She could hear their voices but only recognised occasional words, not enough to make sense of their conversation. They walked together until swallowed by the dark interior.

Alex took additional care as she climbed to the safer and more comfortable position she had spotted. Now was not a good time to drop in on anyone, especially uninvited. She tested the branch below her feet and the one beneath her bottom. Both were strong, though thinner and springier. She was less visible now, and certainly more comfortable.

A raised voice drifted through the gaping doorway. Once more, Alex feared for her brother.

Please, God, please.

In a matter of seconds, two things happened. She detected a slight movement at the rear of the car below. As she watched, the boot lifted cautiously and paused briefly before it rose fully and someone rolled out. A small figure struggled to its feet, lowered the boot carefully, and after a hasty look about, limped away. She watched its progress until foliage interrupted her view.

Next, her eyes flicked up at a blinding flash beyond the roof of the building. A silver car, reflecting flashes of sunlight off its windscreen, was gliding slowly towards her over the uneven grass. A faint tail of dust trailed behind it.

Momentarily, it was hidden by the building before reappearing noiselessly below. It stopped in the shade of the poplars to her right. The triple-point Mercedes symbol on its bonnet glared haughtily at the car squatting before the doorway. A bald man in suit and tie slid out and quietly closed his door behind him.

He paused for a moment to survey his surroundings. For one chilling moment, Alex thought she had been discovered when he turned his face upwards, appearing to look into her tree. As she shrank into the foliage, a shroud of dread descended over her. His Asian features subconsciously linked him with that dead man on Motuarohia Island. His whole being radiated menace. Her fear was affirmed when he reached inside his jacket and withdrew a pistol before turning and walking slowly towards the building.

He stood motionless, gun pointing into the dark void, head to one side, listening. Her heart was thumping so loudly Alex felt he must surely hear it.

'Stop there!' The clipped Asian accent carried clearly above the drumming in her chest. It took a moment before she realised the voice came not from below her tree but from the man now standing in the doorway with his back to her.

Relief was short-lived, however. A movement below turned her insides to water. Someone was climbing her tree. With mounting horror, her eyes followed his every move as he climbed closer and closer. Thoughts of stamping on his hands when he reached her branch, or kicking him in the face, flitted through her head but were instantly dismissed. Even if her weakened limbs could move, there was ultimately no escape.

At the very place she had first perched, he stopped and squatted, motionless, catching his breath and staring intently at the open doorway. He didn't look up, and Alex half entertained the possibility that he was unaware of her. She didn't dare move. Even breathing might betray her.

Muffled voices drifted from the building. She heard the same clipped tones, 'Please, no come. You leave now. Goodbye,' as the Asian man gestured with his pistol in the doorway. Hāmuera's cousin and the big man walked staunchly into the light but threw backward glances nevertheless. The pistol remained levelled at them as Piri lifted then slammed the car boot shut before both men slid into their seats, closing the doors firmly after them.

The motor roared into life, and almost immediately, their car sprang forward, braked, and turned in one sliding motion, before accelerating away in the direction it had come. Satisfied they were gone, the Asian returned the pistol inside his jacket and, after a last glance around, disappeared inside.

The figure perched below now began looking about, apparently undecided as to the next move. His face turned upwards. It was only a side-on glimpse, but for the second time, relief surged through her. It was Hāmuera.

Alex didn't dare speak. At first, he seemed oblivious to her vigorous arm waving, but when his head finally turned in her direction, he jumped so violently at seeing her that his branch bucked up and down. For a moment, he fought for grip and balance. When the branch had stilled, he looked up at her again.

His expression almost made her giggle out loud. Never before had she seen such a mixture of emotions and questioning on one pale face. She put a cautioning finger to her lips. Answers could wait. He gripped a branch above and rose to a standing position.

Immediately a look of pain shot across his face. Alex clapped a hand over her mouth as it became obvious by his rubbing and leg movements that he was experiencing pins and needles. This was almost too much to hold in. Hāmuera didn't understand the suppressed laughter, and his puzzlement grew greater.

There was sufficient room for the two of them, so she signalled for him to join her. He shook his head at first and continued rubbing and flexing before gingerly climbing to her. As he sat beside her, feet firmly planted on the branch below and both hands clutching a thin bough above, Alex noted the tremor in his legs. Either he was afraid of heights or the fright had badly affected him. She leaned close to his ear and whispered, 'Are you OK?'

He nodded. His breath came fast and noisily.

'Do you come here often?' she whispered and tried unsuccessfully to suppress the snort that exploded from her mouth. This was getting crazy. Here they were trespassing, there was a man with a gun below, her brother was in danger of discovery, and she was cracking a funny in a shaky perch ten metres above the ground and less than two seconds from vertical impact. Nevertheless, it broke the extreme tension, and it seemed to work for Hāmuera.

He turned and breathed into her ear, 'Only during the mating season.'

For some reason not known to Alex, this was funny. It was his turn to snort. Being a couple of centimetres away from her ear, the blast acted like laughing gas. Silent laughter wrenched their stomachs, lodged briefly in their throats, then erupted in ongoing explosions that shook the branches. Each time they looked at each other's streaming eyes, there were renewed eruptions.

It was the smell of cigarette smoke that sobered them up. Someone was smoking, quite close. She gripped Hāmuera's arm. His eyes, now serious as they looked into hers, spoke the same warning, and they became as still and silent as the boughs on which they rested.

The drone of honeybees, busy among the pōhutukawa blossoms, soaked up the silence. In the distance, a tui began a recital. Poplar leaves shivered at a playful rush of breeze. High above their tree, above the smattering of cotton-wool clouds, came the faint roar of an aircraft on its invisible descent to Auckland's international airport, carrying expectant tourists and travellers returning home for New Year's Day reunions. Somewhere, an outboard motor accelerated away, and a voice shrilled above it.

It was Hāmuera who finally broke the silence.

'I can't see anyone,' he whispered. 'I'll just go down,' he said, motioning towards his earlier perch, 'and have a squiz from there. Keep watching me. If the coast is clear, I'll signal. Don't want to be caught up a tree. No escape, eh. Need to find somewhere we can hide 'n' run from if we have to.'

'But Samuel's inside there,' Alex whispered with quiet emphasis, pointing at the gaping doorway.

Hāmuera looked confused. 'In there? With those fellas?' He made as if to ask something then added, 'Tell me later.'

He descended extra carefully, halting to hug the trunk while looking around. Alex suspected he hugged more for security than secrecy. It took a while, but once he had reached the lower station, he crouched as before and peered intently through branches and foliage, stretching his neck in all directions without moving his solidly planted feet. He looked up to Alex and indicated that he would continue down and for her to follow.

If he was scared of heights, he was being very brave, Alex thought to herself. In many ways, coming down was worse than going up. At least you could know where to put your feet when climbing up. Coming down, it was by feel and by guess much of the time.

She had concentrated on her own descent, and having reached her original perch, she looked for Hāmuera and was surprised to see him framed between two sloping trunks and a horizontal branch at the base of the tree. He beckoned for her to join him.

It didn't take long once she was able to grab the wide section of sloping trunk and shuffle backward with legs astride. The rough bark was reasonably forgiving, but she wished she had worn her jeans. Her inner thighs felt a little raw by the time her feet reached the soil. She brushed her shorts clean of bark fibres while hastily surveying the scene. Hāmuera looked more like his old self.

'Can't see anyone,' he whispered. 'Best to head to that scrub back there. We can see out from that better than anyone can see in, especially if we get down low. Keep this tree between us and the doorway in case anybody's looking. Follow me.'

He set off at a purposeful pace, doubled over and watchful, like a motorcyclist crouched over his fuel tank. Alex followed. She sensed they were almost there when she bumped into Hāmuera's backside.

'Sorry!' she whispered hoarsely.

Hāmuera didn't respond. She straightened up and came face to face with the surprised Oriental face that had stopped her companion. Before either of them had the thought to escape, the barrel of a handgun filled their eyes. Alex felt blood drain from the roots of her hair. Blotches of black slid across her eyes, and her knees struggled to hold her up.

No words were spoken, but the minimal gestures performed by the gun spoke clearly. They both turned and began to walk back to the corrugated iron wall, to the large hole in it, to the doorway and the darkness beyond it.

'He must have gone for a leak,' began Hāmuera, who fell silent as the gun pressed meaningfully and none too gently between his shoulder blades.

This explained why they hadn't spotted anyone. He must have arrived in the Mercedes but not got out until he needed a smoke. And then he must have gone into the scrub to relieve himself. What abysmal bad luck.

As they approached the doorway, the gunman shouted ahead in a foreign language. The reply from inside needed no interpretation. In any language, it would have said, 'You found what?'

Immediately the voice was joined by the man. Before them stood the bald Asian. Cold eyes fixed on them through narrow slits slashed into an expressionless face. He spoke in his own language to his companion and then in English, he said, 'You, big trouble. Not come here, you know. Now you stay, not go. Very big trouble, OK?'

He suddenly grabbed Alex's hand, spun her around and applied a hold that made her double over and move in whichever direction he chose. As long as she went where he directed, there was little discomfort, but if she was too slow to respond, an excruciating pain shot up an arm. A sudden cry informed her that Hāmuera was close behind, held in the same manner by the Asian's accomplice.

Their eyes were barely accustomed to the dim light when they stopped before a door in an inner wall, where she was handed over to the second man, who held her with one hand while still holding Hāmuera with the other. So effective was the hold that neither of them could resist without fierce pain immediately changing their minds.

The door opened. There was more light this side of the wall, but there was little chance of seeing much more than the maze of hay bales they were steered through and a huge multi-wheeled trailer bearing a rigid-hull inflatable boat with two enormous outboard motors hanging off its stern, before another door was pushed open. It revealed what appeared to be an implement shed and workshop.

They were shoved roughly towards the far wall, where an array of farm tools hung on pegs and holders. By the time the men locked the door behind them and their voices receded into the hay bales, Alex and Hāmuera knew the bindings that lashed their hands to the wall removed any chance of escape even if they chose to ignore the threat the Asian had made.

The simple drawing of one finger across his throat conveyed a significant and frightening message.

Chapter 14

Pāua

The rear door of the truck was opened at the gesture of Mr Liu, and although Samuel could see inside, he could not make out what it contained. Wreaths of smoke obscured his view, escaping like special-effects fog at a stage show. Then it dawned on him that it was steam from a large refrigerated compartment.

Colin disappeared into the fog and reappeared, carrying two cartons, which he arranged carefully alongside each other on the edge of the truck floor.

'Here y'are, Mr Liu. All good condition. You look. Extra young, very tender pāua. Best quality.' He spoke in a loud, slow voice, trying to capture the Asian's accent as if to make it easier for him to understand.

The Asian moved forward as Colin lifted the top flaps of each carton. He reached inside the first and, with some difficulty, extracted a bundle in a plastic bag. He vigorously wiped at the icy covering to reveal the contents, which he inspected closely, turning the bag several times. He nodded and removed a similar-sized bag from the second carton. This inspection seemed to please him also.

'Good,' he said. 'Now take.'

Samuel pressed himself flat as the Asian pointed towards where he was lying. Colin picked up one carton and followed him.

'You get the other one, Sid,' he called over his shoulder.

'Not likely, mate,' came the reply. 'I'm just the driver, remember? If we get done for this, I didn't even know what we were carrying, eh. Like, "I wouldn't have driven illegal freight if I'd of known, Your Honour."' He spoke with a mock innocence. 'Me, I just sat in the cab, Your Honour, as it was nothin' ta do with me what they were deliverin'.' He gave a laugh.

'Come on, ya lazy bastard,' Colin replied. 'You're in this up to your fat neck. No judge'll believe that lot of cock and bull. Pull your weight—you've got enough of it.'

Sid laughed again, climbed clumsily into the compartment, and began stacking cartons on the edge of the tray.

Samuel heard the sound of a door opening below him and a slight thud. He pictured a carton being stowed in what must surely be a refrigerated room, perhaps like the one he had seen in the kitchen at youth camp last year.

For some time, cartons of identical size were transferred from truck to chiller room until Colin, lifting his cap and wiping his brow with his forearm, spoke again.

'There y'are, Mr Liu, forty boxes, all good pāua. You pay now? OK?'

At that very moment, a voice called from outside, and Mr Liu questioned back. He walked quickly towards the opening, and as Samuel looked, three figures walked into view, one man and two smaller shapes.

A bag of cement dropped in Samuel's stomach as he recognised first his sister and then the second figure. He could not comprehend how Hāmuera was there. He could comprehend, however, that they were prisoners of a man holding a gun.

Samuel winced as Alex was grabbed and held in a plainly painful hold by Mr Liu. Hāmuera tried to resist as the second man twisted his arm, but his protest was useless. Leaning forward under their holds, both were steered towards the door through which he had so recently sought to escape.

For a short while, the second man, whom Samuel now saw was also Asian, held the two of them while Mr Liu inserted a key in the lock and pushed the door open. The next moment, they were gone.

'This is not looking too good, mate. Crime and kids mean complications. Where did *they* come from?' Sid said.

'Doesn't *matter* where they came from, Col. No jury is gonna b'lieve us if *kids* are involved. We better get the hell out of here b'fore we get any more involved, eh.'

Things had happened so unexpectedly that Colin and Sid, in their bewilderment, had not thought to shut either the chiller door or the door to the truck's compartment. Samuel heard them each slam a door shut and make for the cab of their truck. They paused.

'We gotta get paid though. Get the dough, then go,' said Colin. 'We've taken enough risk getting the stuff here. May as well get the reward.'

Sid climbed into the driver's seat. Colin stood beside his open door and fumbled for a cigarette. He lit it and puffed rapidly three or four times before drawing deeply into his lungs.

Sid's voice leaked out of the cab. 'Reckon I could do with one of those now.'

Colin pulled another from the pack, put it to his mouth, and lit it from his own cigarette before handing it into the cab.

From his rooftop position, Samuel was unable to see inside the cab, but he presumed Sid would be looking in his wing mirror at the door in the wall behind him, eager to start the motor the moment the Asians appeared.

He wasn't wrong.

'Here they are,' he called, and the motor instantly burbled.

Samuel watched Colin walk around and begin talking to the two men, but he was unable to hear their conversation over the clacking of the diesel injectors.

Colin received an envelope, opened it, and quickly counted a wedge of banknotes. There was something clearly wrong. He began to argue. The result was rapid and final. A handgun pointing centimetres from his chest settled the deal, and Colin, walking backward to the truck, turned and leapt for his door. For the second time that afternoon, a vehicle left in great haste.

Once the departing truck had faded into the distance, silence fell as thick as a blanket. Although increasingly uncomfortable lying on his stomach, in the space of an hour, Samuel had seen sufficient to know that one careless move could mean capture. Everything he did from now on must be carefully thought through and just as carefully preformed. He instinctively understood it was not just *his* well-being at risk. Alex and Hāmuera depended upon him also.

Caution controlled every action. He had to know if the two men were still there. Silence didn't necessarily mean he was alone. Eventually, sure that he was alone, he sat up.

He was surprised at how stiff his limbs had become. He was dusting his clothes off, revelling in the relief afforded by standing, when he heard their voices again.

Resuming his now-familiar flattened position, he watched the two Asians as they filed through the small door, heading straight for the wide opening. Perhaps they were leaving. He hoped so, desperately hoped so.

Because they left the main door open, Samuel realised their return was certain. A major decision had to be made. He had to be sure his sister and Hāmuera were all right.

Briefly his imagination took over and he pictured two lifeless bodies lying on the ground. He shook the image from his head. They needed to be alive, and he needed to release them or get help if that was impossible.

His mind was made up. As quickly as his protesting limbs allowed, he slid off the chiller roof, climbed down the framing, and slunk along the wall, keeping one eye on the slab of daylight through which the Asians had passed.

He reached the small door without sign of their return, and slipping through, he was instantly grateful for how much more light there was on that side.

After one false turn, he found his way through the maze of hay bales and stared at a magnificent boat, its massive trailer parked in readiness to be attached to a blue tractor standing on a concrete pad that extended under the huge doors.

He swept the scene with eager eyes. At least three more boats and tractors of similar size could have occupied the floor. In fact, it could easily have been a small aeroplane or helicopter hangar.

To his right and against the wall, a roofless four-metre-long wooden enclosure provided the only possibility where prisoners might be held. The door at its near end was closed, but as he crept closer, he spotted an old-fashioned key projecting from it. This was one bit of good fortune in a day where things had gone from bad to worse and until now had promised to plunge into disaster.

'Alex.'

His hoarse whisper was swallowed in the vastness.

'Alex, are you in there?' This time from beside the door.

'Samuel,' Alex blurted with a mixture of relief and fear. 'Those men have guns, and they will use them. You've got to go for help.'

'They've tied us up, ehōa. Can you get in here?' Hāmuera called.

'I think so. The key's in the door. Hold on a minute.'

Samuel tried the handle and pulled. It wouldn't open, but when he turned the key, it easily clicked and the door swung smoothly towards him. At that very moment, he caught the sound of voices.

'Oh no! Gotta hide! They're coming back.'

Making an instant decision, he scampered as fast as his legs would take him and lunged towards the nearest wall of hay bales, flinging arms and legs in desperate search of holds. The hay proved both slippery and prickly. Prickly was of no consequence under the circumstances, but slippery increased his panic as he fought for hand and toe grip.

After several agonising slips backward and fighting with a bale that teetered and almost tumbled upon him, he reached the top of the stack and fell headfirst into a cavity. He lay there, panting as quietly as his heaving lungs allowed until the panting subsided, listening with the focus that survival demands.

No sound. No movement. Nothing. A silent world, bound by walls once lush and sweet in summer fields. He felt strangely safe. In another world, another time. A corrugated sky above, warm air surrounding. Under other conditions, he could have fallen asleep, lulled by the warmth and quiet.

How long he had lain there when startled by the tractor motor he was unsure. At the first grinding of the starter motor, his stomach had tensed, but once the motor began its regular rumble and he realised what was happening, he carefully raised his head and peered over the bales.

The new man sat upon the tractor seat, one hand on the gearstick and the other on the steering wheel. He seemed unfamiliar with the machine, for he was having difficulty finding the correct gear. The tractor lurched backward and almost immediately halted while he fought the gear lever again. This time, it moved slowly forward, and he steered it in a tight circle before straightening up and driving towards Samuel.

He ducked his head and kept low for some time as the motor described various manoeuvres. When the sound suggested it had moved further away, he cautiously took a peek.

The trailer had been attached to the tractor, and the boat was reversing on a weaving course to where the tractor had originally stood. The driver was not skilled at backing, and now Mr Liu emerged from somewhere to guide with hand signals. Eventually it backed almost to the large doors, and following a few shouted instructions, the motor puttered to silence.

Mr Liu was unhappy about something. Although his language was foreign, it became apparent to Samuel by his repeated gestures and actions that Mr Liu had found the door where the two prisoners were held unlocked and open, and he blamed his companion, who was denying everything with counter-gestures and acting. Their voices became more animated and loud.

Finally, Mr Liu shouted an order. The other man bowed a stiff bow and quickly moved to the door. He shut it firmly, turned the lock, tested it, and removed the key, which he pocketed. He followed Mr Liu's departing form and was quickly lost in the wall of bales.

Samuel turned and faced the separating wall, wondering if he could see them pass through the door. The door was not visible, but he saw two bobbing heads briefly above some lower bales and then they were gone.

Chapter 15

Imprisoned

Silence followed intense discussion about Samuel. They heard no voices themselves despite their prison being roofless and the door being left ajar by his rapid departure. However, as he hadn't returned and no alarm was raised, they figured he must have successfully hidden.

Hāmuera whispered instructions on how to ease the discomfort of the twine that held them securely to the wall and then they sat mute for some time, listening.

'How're your hands now?' Hāmuera's voice came like an unexpected splash of water.

'Better, thanks.'

Silence.

'What are they going to do to us? What's going on?' There was a quaver in her voice.

'I think they didn't like us coming to their party without an invitation. We should've brought a present, eh.'

Alex became agitated. 'Don't kid around, Hāmuera, we're in serious trouble. They could *kill* us. I've never had a gun pointed at me before. Have you?'

Both became engrossed in their own thoughts until the sudden starting of a nearby motor jolted them alert. For the next little while, the motor revved, idled, changed gear, grew louder or softer, and they could only imagine what was happening beyond their restricted vision.

When the motor ceased, Alex's stomach tensed. Raised voices could now be heard, and although they were in another language, she was certain they were arguing. They both jumped as the door to their prison was slammed shut. A key turned in the lock, and faint footsteps faded quickly.

Alex eventually broke the silence. 'Why did you come here, Hāmuera?'

He turned his head and looked soberly at her before speaking. 'Well, I thought I knew what was going down, but now I'm not so sure. I hitched a ride in Piri's car, only he didn't know it, of course. I knew he was up to something with that gang he hangs around with, 'cause there've been some pretty heavy bros at my aunty's place this week. I thought it was about dope 'cause . . .' He hesitated. 'Well, you might as well know. Piri's been growing it on your land. Kiriana let it slip, but she made me promise not to tell.'

'I know. I saw it.'

'You did?' He looked strangely at her.

'Yeah, I did. Who's Kiriana, then?'

'She's another cousin. She's five years older than me. Got into a bit of trouble down in Hamilton, so they sent her up here to get away from bad company.' He laughed ironically. 'So she meets up with Piri and she's got even badder company. Crazy, eh?'

Alex thought for a moment. 'Did you know our house had been broken into?' she asked.

'Kiriana told me.'

'How did she know?'

'I suppose it doesn't matter if you know now. She bragged about how clever she was. She made big eyes at this guy working for an electrician up here, and he fell for her big time. She's a good-looker, and he thought she was pretty cool, coming from Hamilton and that. He told her he could get into lots of the houses they did work on because he knew where people left their keys. I think he wanted to take her into one of them . . . you know,' he added awkwardly.

Alex ignored the implication.

'So she found out from him where we hide *our* key.' This was a statement rather than a question. Things were beginning to fall into place. 'So once she got in, she smashed the glass to make it look like someone had broken in and put the key back. That way, the lock might not get changed when the door was repaired, so she could get in again at some later time.'

'That's pretty much what she told me. You're not just a pretty face, are you, Alexandra?' Despite their situation, it made her feel quite fluttery inside.

She gathered her thoughts and then, as further pieces of the jigsaw slotted into place, she continued. 'So *she* took the food and drink because *she* was the one who stayed up in the obs. post.'

Hāmuera looked blank. 'Observation post . . . lookout . . . tree hut,' she explained.

'Oh, right. Kiriana bragged about that too. She said she could see and hear everything and tell Piri on her cell phone. He said he would pay her fifty dollars a day when the stuff was sold, so she was keen—specially as she could just lie around all day.'

'So she was there when the police came. She must have called Piri and he said to phone him the moment the coast was clear, and while we were in Russell, he got a couple of mates to help him cut the marijuana and take it down to the beach. And they used our dinghy to get it over to this place.'

Hāmuera looked astonished. 'You're amazing, you know that, Alexandra? You worked it out all on your own. I only know because I listened to Piri and his mates when they were having some beers afterwards. They didn't know I could hear. And it's just like you said.'

Alex glowed with satisfaction. It was all coming clear now.

'But', she continued, 'they couldn't get it all out to the boat by the time we returned, so they hid some of it nearby to be picked up next time we cleared out, right?'

'I wouldn't know anything about that,' Hāmuera said, but the way he said it slotted another jigsaw piece into place.

'That's when you borrowed our dinghy, wasn't it, Hāmuera? *You* took the rest of it in our boat that night.'

Hāmuera didn't answer straight away.

'It's not like you think, Alexandra. I'm not like them, eh. Heaps of guys at school think it's cool to smoke dope. I tried it a couple of times, but I've seen how it ruined my dad so he couldn't keep a job. My mum had two jobs to pay our rent and food and stuff. They got into a fight over it. Dad ended up in the slammer for a month for belting Mum. I didn't touch a joint after that, eh. I've seen the sort of people that are the biggies too. You don't mess with them. Piri thinks he's tough and staunch, but he's not. Not like the ones in Auckland. They are some mean dudes.'

Alex believed him. 'What did you do with the . . . er, dope that night, then?'

'I went to my nana's.'

'When I challenged you, you agreed you had lied.'

'I know. I did though. I heard where the stuff had been hidden, and I took some of it to prove to Nana what Piri was up to. I kicked myself after telling you I was going to see her. I didn't want her to get involved in anyone's thinking. She didn't believe Piri was into that sort of thing, you know, growing and dealing. She just thought he got on the beer with his mates and had a joint from time to time like most of them do up here.'

An irrelevant thought flashed into her mind. 'Your nana wears a pink hat, doesn't she?'

Hāmuera looked at her and smiled. 'That's bizarre. How do you know that?'

'She was in the car the first day I saw you. I bet she was telling him off for the way he was driving.'

'Too right. She really ripped into him, eh. And when he blew the radiator, she told him it served him right.'

'She sounds a good sort.'

'She's the best. Ugly, eh. No teeth. Face like a dried fish. Plenty of heart though. She's not scared of anybody, and she tells things like they are. Piri is respectful of her 'cause she doesn't let him get away with anything even though he's thirty-something.'

'Our dinghy,' Alex began. 'What happened to it?'

'Nana said I had to stay the night 'cause it was too rough to row back. She thought I was sleeping in the garage, but I didn't want you to get into trouble. I nearly made it all the way, then this wicked wave tipped me out not far from your beach. I grabbed the oars and kicked in to shore with them. I couldn't find the boat in the dark, so I came back early in the morning. You know the rest.'

Alex nodded thoughtfully. It seemed she had almost completed a jigsaw, but some extra pieces belonging to a different puzzle had mysteriously appeared, a puzzle that included the Asians.

A man in a green surgical gown and mask was about to cut off her hands. A pink hat perched above his slanted eyes. A sinister curved sword appeared in his hands, and he ordered her not to cry if it hurt or he would cut off her head also. The blade gleamed briefly as he raised it above his head before swiftly bringing it down across both her wrists.

Alex cried out as she awoke. Her heart raced as she fought to make sense of her surroundings. Her wrists hurt, and it took some effort to accept that her hands were still attached.

'Bad dream?'

Hāmuera's words brought her rapidly into the present.

'Yeah,' she conceded, her breath coming in short gasps. 'My hands were being cut off.'

As her breathing returned to normal, she noted how much darker it had become.

'Have I been asleep long? What time is it, do you think?'

'About two hours past tucker time by my belly reckoning. Say half past seven or eight o'clock.'

'I bet Dad will be looking for us by now. He's a detective. He'll catch these guys.'

'You never told me he was a detective,' said Hāmuera in surprise.

She was about to respond when a thought suddenly entered her head. 'Samuel? Anything more from Samuel?' she asked.

Hāmuera shook his head. 'He's probably got away. That'll be what's happened. Probably got your father on the way here by now.'

That was a brighter possibility than his capture, and Alex felt heartened. It wouldn't be long now and they would be rescued and those men would be locked up. Another Mr Asia captured, this time by her father.

She breathed in relief. 'Yes, I think you're right. Won't be long now.'

Almost immediately there came the sound of voices. New voices. Rescue was imminent and so quickly.

'What did I just say? They're here. We're going to be OK,' Alex whispered with increasing delight.

'Dad, we're in here,' she shouted repeatedly at the top of her voice.

The next moment, voices sounded just beyond the wall. The key rattled in the lock, and the door burst open.

Alex could not recognise faces in the dim light, but suddenly, a light flicked on to reveal two European faces, neither of which she recognised, flanked by the two Asians.

'What the blazes are we going to do with the kids, then?' said the taller of the two to no one in particular. They stared briefly at them without moving from the doorway.

The bald Asian said something in his own language, and his companion cackled.

'What'd he say?' the man asked.

'Boss say, food for pāua. Drop in sea. Good idea.' He laughed again.

The second European said, 'Hey, Dan, this thing is getting too heavy. We said we'd take the stuff in the boat. That's what we're paid for. I'm not having nothing to do with killing, 'specially if it's kids, no way, man.' He turned with the last words to face Mr Asia.

Mr Asia just smiled coldly and said, 'They come, OK? Not stop job, OK? No problem. I fix.'

Dan spoke softly. 'We'll do the job, Mr Liu, but no kids, OK?' He tried to outstare the Asian, but he was the first to lower his eyes. He continued in a less-sure voice. 'We'll get the stuff loaded, and we can discuss this later.'

Then turning to his companion, he ordered, 'Come on, Travis, let's do it. We have a rendezvous to keep.'

The two turned and disappeared through the doorway.

Mr Asia took a long look at the prisoners before speaking at some length to the other man, who nodded, a wide smile spreading across his features. They both laughed and left, locking the door behind them.

A chill snaked down Alex's spine.

Chapter 16

Night Run

Lights like four large glow-worms hung from the roof, illuminating the concrete pad. The two recent arrivals trekked back and forth, carrying cartons from the chiller room to the boat. A small set of steps gave access to the stern, where Mr Liu's accomplice received each carton to stack it carefully against the rigid hull, ten cartons to a row, two rows high against each hull.

In the shadowy area above the lights, Samuel could afford to be less cautious. From his elevated position, it was like watching a movie, a movie in which he had no desire to become a central character.

Earlier, he had cautiously left his haven to spy out his chances of escaping. He had practically walked into the back of Mr Liu, who was seated on a cheap plastic chair just beyond the door through the centre wall. He had frozen for a moment, petrified that he might be discovered, but a low rumbling and rhythmic movement assured him the man was sleeping.

The adrenalin rush left him with weak knees and a strong resolve not to push his luck any further. Although the man had been asleep, he felt sure that if the man was wakened, a bullet would overtake him in a fraction of a second. Under the circumstances, he was content to remain in the safety of his hideaway despite Alex and Hāmuera's situation. Their best chance was for him to remain hidden until he could safely escape to get help.

The cartons were stacked and secured with ties by the time Mr Liu appeared under the lights. He carried a handheld radio device with a whip aerial in one hand and, seeing the loading was completed, commenced talking into it. He barked out some instructions to his accomplice, who obediently took out a flip-top notebook and began writing.

Samuel could not hear what was said, and it would have meant nothing to him even if he could. He guessed it concerned whoever was waiting for the frozen pāua.

A sudden burst of activity began. Travis swung into the tractor seat and fumbled with the ignition as the large doors leading out to the launching ramp and Manawaora Bay were swung wide one by one. Dan walked into the light, a faint hue of fading dusk behind him. The tractor growled, roared, and began to reverse trailer and boat through the yawning gap. Dan remained beside the doors, watching the tractor until the twin outboard motors tracked into the gloom.

The two Asians observed from where they stood, but once the boat had disappeared, they began walking purposefully to the implement shed. Samuel barely breathed. As they neared the door, Dan's voice pierced the brittle silence.

'Mr Liu! No kids, OK?'

The two continued, oblivious to the voice.

'Mr Liu, you hear me? Leave the kids alone. Leave them here. I'll deal with them when we get back.' Dan's pleading was tinged with warning.

There was nothing to suggest they had heard. Instead, they unlocked the door and disappeared inside. As there was no roof to the shed, Samuel caught smudged glimpses of the tops of their heads but was unable to see anything of Alex or Hāmuera until they emerged through the doorway and into the light.

Their hands were tied behind their backs. Both appeared unsteady on their feet, Alex looking helpless, frightened, like a kitten released into new surroundings, Hāmuera more like a puppy anticipating a smack for a naughty act. His head leaned away from his captors, his legs ready to evade a disciplinary hand.

Dan came to meet them. 'Come on, Mr Liu. That's kidnapping. I won't take the kids. Do you understand me?'

He stood in front of Mr Liu, arms stretched forward and wide to reinforce his plea. Despite the distance, Samuel sensed a coiled spring inside Dan's tense body. A coiled spring poised on a hair trigger.

Mr Liu moved so quickly it was impossible to tell what he did. There were three sharp sounds in rapid succession. A shriek of pain rebounded like a snooker ball off the walls as Dan crumpled forward. He remained on the ground, unmoving.

Alex and Hāmuera stood transfixed, their faces a blend of disbelief and horror. Mr Liu clasped his hands together, cracked his knuckles, then laughed dismissively at the sprawled figure at his feet. He delivered a further instruction to his henchman, who disappeared briefly into the shed before returning with an unravelling coil of binding twine. He then set about binding Dan's hands and feet.

Samuel's heart pounded so loudly he could barely think. It was plain that these ruthless men were taking his sister and Hāmuera away and their lives were in deadly danger. He watched helplessly as they were marched beyond the lights, into the gullet of the night.

A strong light cut like a laser beam through the darkness. Not knowing where she was going added to Alex's extreme anxiety, and now they were heading down the boat ramp towards a blinding light. By lowering her head, she could just make out the twin hulls of the boat below the light. It had been launched and now faced the boat ramp in readiness to take on its passengers.

Travis, who had been somewhere behind the light, now knelt on the bow, and lowering a small stainless-steel ladder, which ground gently at the water's edge, he assisted Mr Liu aboard. The operation was achieved without him wetting his shoes.

Travis looked unsettled. 'Where's Dan?' he asked after Mr Liu.

'Not come,' came the reply.

Travis looked more unsettled. 'What's the problem, then? Why's he not coming?'

Alex was about to blurt out something when Hāmuera's voice came from behind her, 'They gave him the bash. Just do as they say or you'll get the—'

The next moment, Alex was jolted in the back as Hāmuera collided into her. Quickly regaining her balance, she realised that he had been shoved violently from behind. The accompanying words were foreign, but there was no doubting their meaning.

'Hey, cut it out, Ching! Pick on someone your own size.' Hāmuera was angry. He wasn't going to take this treatment without protest. He cursed under his breath.

Travis reached down to help her up the ladder. It was almost impossible on her own with her hands tied behind her back. He steadied her by the shoulders, and as she neared the last rung, he pulled her towards him in a bear hug. To any observer, it would have seemed a necessary action to balance her.

'Take it easy, girl. Don't do anything silly. I'll look after you,' he whispered in one ear. Having steadied her, he steered her through an opening in the Perspex screen into the interior of the boat. There she made out the shape of a bench seat and sank on to it, glad for the padded squab beneath her.

Hāmuera followed, stumbled, and almost sat on her lap.

'Sorry,' he mumbled. 'Accident.' Then his humour returned briefly. 'Might enjoy it next time, eh.'

Alex smiled in the dark despite herself. If she was in trouble, Hāmuera was a good friend to be with. *We are in trouble. And he is a friend.* She surprised herself with this silent acknowledgement.

Travis stood silhouetted on the bow, waiting. After a short wait, the darkness deepened, and Alex realised that the lights in the building had been turned off.

Eventually, the Asian lieutenant clambered through the Perspex and felt his way to the bench seat, wedging himself beside Alex. The smell of stale perspiration and Eastern food enveloped her, and his physical presence dominated like a stone wall. She shuffled slightly along the seat to increase the space between them and felt somewhat comforted when her thigh rested against Hāmuera's.

Travis closed the gap in the Perspex screen and took his place before the controls. The spotlight was turned off. There was the slightest of tremors, and the boat moved slowly backward into deeper water before, at the command of the wheel, it turned on a course towards Motuarohia Island.

As Alex's eyes adjusted to the minimal light in the night sky, a myriad stars pricked through deep-blue velvet, causing the land mass on either side to mount from the sea.

Travis edged the throttle forward. It was remarkable how little noise the twin outboards made and how little wake the twin hulls left, though stirring up twin trails of fluorescence as they hugged the western shore of Manawaora Bay.

To their right, Alex and Hāmuera gazed at the tiny light filtering through trees in Clendon Cove. *What's happening at the bach? Dad will be searching, must be. Has Samuel got there yet, told them where we were—what happened? Mum must be worried sick. If Samuel told them about the boat, they might be on the lookout for it.* Even as she thought these things, Alex knew there was little hope. This boat was muscular, chosen for its speed and manoeuvrability. Drug running was high risk. Runners needed to outrun the authorities if discovered.

As if to prove the point, the motors' pitch rose and the bow lifted as the twin props savagely ejected the water in a flurry of fluorescence many metres behind. Spray scattered on either side as mast headlights in Ōrokawa slid swiftly by and then stuttered behind the black mass of the point. They foamed close by the rocky outcrop of Bateman Island before adjusting course for the gap between Motuarohia and Moturua Islands. Beyond lay the open sea and, as she soon discovered, open throttle.

When the lights went out, Samuel fought the compulsion to yell. To yell for fear, for Mum, for the lights to be turned on again, for it all to go away. But the greater fear of being captured, and the conviction that Alex must be rescued, cemented his teeth together.

Stars gradually smeared the clear roof panels, making them glow dimly in the dark arch overhead. Gradually, his eyes gained their night vision, and bulky shapes formed. He had both legs over the bales, ready to slide to the ground when he heard the cough. He froze. A further cough was followed by a groan. A long, drawn-out groan. The hairs on his head settled as he figured the sounds came from the man felled by Mr Liu.

Once on solid ground, he made his way easily enough towards the injured man, guided by his occasional groans. His vague outline came into focus, and Samuel crouched beside him.

'Mister, are you OK?' He reached out and touched Dan's shoulder. 'Hey, mister, can you speak?'

Dan stiffened. 'Who . . . What happened? I can't see,' he croaked.

'I'm Samuel. You got belted by that Chinese man, remember?'

'Yeah,' he whispered.

He attempted to sit up and flopped to the ground again.

'My arms—legs won't work.' His voice became stronger with an edge of panic.

'You're tied up, that's why,' said Samuel. The humour of the situation would be released in the retelling later.

'Got a knife,' Dan said.

'No. I haven't got anything,' Samuel said.

'No. I got a knife. My pocket,' Dan explained, his voice slightly stronger.

Samuel felt for Dan's belt and moved his hands down his thigh, feeling for the solid shape of a knife. Nothing.

'Other pocket,' Dan said, more in control of his thoughts now. 'Roll over on my other side. Give . . . me a . . . hand, will you?'

The task was not easy with Dan's hands trussed behind his back. Nor did the dark help. Samuel ran his hand down Dan's newly offered leg, and this time, the hard bulk of a pocketknife filled his palm. Samuel discovered that pockets are designed more for the wearer to get into than others.

'Hands first,' Dan instructed as the main blade was successfully drawn from the safety of the handle. 'Careful.'

The warning was not needed, but Samuel recognised that Dan's mind was beginning to function well. Physical improvement would take more time, he guessed. He felt his way to the bonds and carefully sawed at the twine, relieved that it took minimal effort to cut through. Dan's hands suddenly parted, and he could hear him rubbing them together gently at first and then with greater freedom.

'Oh, mate, that feels good!' Samuel could imagine the expression on his face. 'I'll do my feet. Where's the knife?'

Samuel offered it in the dark and was dismayed at the cry from Dan. 'Not blade first, boy. Don't you know knife safety?' He paused. 'How old are you? Thirteen, fourteen?'

'Nearly ten, and I'm really sorry,' Samuel replied repentantly.

'You're a big boy for that age. You looked much older with the girl.'

For a moment, Samuel was confused then he said, 'That was Hāmuera with my sister.'

It was Dan's turn to be confused. 'But there were just two of you, weren't there?'

'They didn't know I was here. I was hiding up in the hay.'

'So', said Dan, his voice stronger but tinged with suspicion as he cut the twine around his ankles, 'what did you see?'

Samuel relayed everything, and when he came to the description of what happened after Dan tried to prevent Alex and Hāmuera being taken, Dan interrupted tersely.

'They took the kids, then! OK, I've got to stop them, and you've got to help me. The fishing boat won't want the kids on board, and Mr Liu won't want to bring them back because . . .' His voice faded away. 'What I mean is there's a hell of a lot of money involved with pāua smuggling. Mr Liu has invested . . .'

After a short pause, he spoke rapidly. 'I don't care if I get done for this, but I'm not going to be party to kids . . .' Again his voice faded.

'I know where the light switches are,' Samuel interrupted. 'Do you want me to turn them on?'

'Good man!' Dan said, pushing awkwardly to his feet.

Samuel's eyes had fully adjusted to the dark, so it was not difficult to find where the movie set had been plunged into darkness. He flicked all four switches down in one sweep of his hand. Reassuring light instantly revealed the concrete strip and Dan shielding his eyes.

'OK, we've got to get to a telephone. Where's the nearest house . . . what's your name again?' Dan asked.

'It's Samuel, and my dad's got a telephone, and we live just across the bay, and I've got a boat we can row there.'

'My car is out the back. We can drive there, can't we?' Dan inquired.

At Samuel's nod, he began gingerly walking towards the open door. Although his body ached, the urgency of the situation pushed his discomfort into the background. At the doors, he diverted to the light switches, and for the second time that night, pitch black filled the place.

'They'll put the lights on when they get back. That could be useful to know,' he said.

Samuel thought so too.

The sea was smooth and gun-metal dark in the shelter of the islands, but a small swell met them as they sped into the open ocean. Travis stood at the wheel, enclosed by the curved Perspex screen. The dimmed instrument panel glowed with blurry red circles. He thrust the throttle lever as far forward as it would go and the motors responded with a muffled scream. Alex and Hāmuera fought for balance as the bow tilted skywards momentarily before lunging aggressively at the slim silver line of the ocean horizon.

With each passing minute, fear thrust its roots deeper into every nerve and sinew until Alex could barely breathe. When she spoke, her stomach quivered like shivery grass.

'What are they going to do to us?'

Hāmuera sat with shoulders hunched forward in deep concentration and appeared not to have heard. Alex began to repeat the question when a subtle shake of his head stopped her. After what seemed an age, he spoke softly, still looking ahead.

'They're going to meet a boat and give them what's in these boxes.' He nodded towards the cartons on either side of them.

Alex had already guessed the cartons were the reason for the night run, but it was so different from how she imagined marijuana would be packaged. Besides, there was so much of it. In the end, she had given up trying to make sense of it all until now.

'It's not marijuana, is it?' she stated.

'Nah. These boxes are damned cold. They've got frozen stuff in them, eh. I'm trying not to lean on them.'

Alex blinked hard and searched her mind for anything that would link criminals and big money with frozen stuff in cartons. There was nothing.

'What's in them, then?'

'Pāua, I reckon.'

Alex puzzled for a moment. Pāua shell was made into all sorts of souvenirs for tourists, but it didn't need to be frozen.

'It's a delic . . . something Chinese and Japanese people like to eat. Piri said it's black abalone, and I think they pay heaps for it,' Hāmuera continued.

So it wasn't the shell, but the meat inside. She remained locked in thought. What possessed their captors to skim the ocean at breakneck speed to deliver frozen shellfish to a boat at night was just beginning to make sense.

'But what are they going to do to us, Hāmuera?' she repeated.

'Wish I knew,' he replied, but at the same time, he wondered whether he really did want to know. The Asian had said something about them being food for pāua. His laugh and the expression on his face flashed into his head. 'Probably want to keep an eye on us until they've finished the job.'

Alex considered this before asking quietly, 'Then what?'

Hāmuera shrugged. Her only hope was what Travis had whispered in her ear as she came aboard. 'I'll look after you,' he had said. Despite the action caused by the ocean swell at the speed they were travelling and the discomfort of her tied hands, she dozed.

She came to with her head on Hāmuera's shoulder as the motors began to slow. Mr Liu, speaking into his handheld radio, stood alongside Travis. The communication was brief. A short treble response hissed from the radio, and he signalled a half circle as he spoke to Travis.

Hāmuera pressed her into an upright position from where she lay against him.

'You've given me the cold shoulder,' he quipped.

It took a moment before she understood what he meant. 'I'm sorry,' she stammered. 'I went to sleep and I didn't . . . are you OK?'

The motors slowed further, and the boat ceased to plane. A short time later, several orange lights appeared then disappeared again as the craft rocked gently on its wake. As the outboard motors came to idle, she felt the rumbling engines before she heard them. The dark bulk of a large vessel loomed beside them, and she caught sight of several indistinct faces looking down at them.

Mr Liu directed a light onto the rusting side of the ship. Foreign letters and the number 27 briefly appeared and then a rope ladder thudded onto the cartons beside Hāmuera.

Their journey was over.

Chapter 17

Trawler

Travis took a firm hold on a rung of the rope ladder and pulled the craft close to the trawler. Two further ropes snaked down, thudding heavily near the stern. Mr Liu gave abrupt orders to his accomplice, who clambered swiftly to gather them. He part coiled one before throwing it forward to Travis, who expertly secured it to a fitting near the bow. The other he twisted around a solid ring attached to the near-side pontoon.

This done, Mr Liu with one foot on the ladder spoke again to his accomplice, who grinned and pulled a handgun from his belt. He waved it in the air before returning it. The point was made. If there was trouble, the gun would set matters right.

The rope ladder jiggled as Mr Liu clambered upwards and disappeared aboard.

Shortly, a mesh sling appeared above them. The languid swell lifted and dropped them against the rumbling iron of the trawler. As they rose on a swell, Travis seized the sling, and shuffling past Alex, he drew it down upon the floor behind them.

He began removing the securing ties from the stacked cartons. As soon as they were freed, he began carrying them to the flattened mesh. A pile of cartons soon filled the netting. The lieutenant yelled something unintelligible and signalled for it to be raised. The sling rose slowly, a swollen black hole in the orange light, until it disappeared on board. A short time later, it reappeared like a drooping spider web floating through amber haze to the floor again.

Alex and Hāmuera watched each sling load disappear with mounting apprehension. As the craft grew lighter, Alex's heart became heavier. She sensed that nothing would happen until the last carton had been hoisted into the trawler. But after that . . .

'I'm gonna take him out,' Hāmuera whispered in her ear. His fierceness surprised her.

'What?' Alex felt an unexpected thrill course through her body.

'If he frees our hands, he'll free you first 'cause you're not a threat. You distract him and I'll fix him.'

'What do I do?' Alex whispered back.

'I don't know, eh,' he hissed. The tension showed. 'Make a fuss about... pins and needles or something, but wait till my hands are free. OK?'

Alex nodded and her stomach drew tight. She calculated it to be eleven o'clock or thereabouts, but she felt more awake now than she had all day, a combination of adrenalin and primal instinct. The helplessness and dread that had clung to her like a damp wet-suit yielded to hope.

Travis was taking cartons from the second row now, working his way closer towards them. As he drew alongside Hāmuera, he muttered something. He didn't look at Hāmuera, who appeared to have heard nothing.

Travis lifted another carton and turned for the sling. Alex looked intently at Hāmuera, who gazed straight ahead. He waited until the Asian watched the sling being hoisted aloft.

'You reckon you can drive this boat?'

'What?' Alex choked.

'Just be ready. Don't wait for anybody.'

'But—'

Hāmuera's knee signalled her to stop. The accomplice was looking in their direction.

'Be good, no trouble.' He scowled. 'I make hands good, you be good, OK?' He patted the bulge of the handgun.

The last of the cartons was stacked in the mesh, and as it rose for the final time, the Asian walked purposefully over to them, adjusting his balance with each swell that lifted then slid under the craft.

The blade glinted steely orange in the trawler's suspended light. Dread screamed up from some dark recess as she twisted violently away, but his hand grasped behind her neck, and in an instant, she had been pulled forward and turned. Her back quivered, anticipating the cold blade plunging between her ribs.

Her quivering continued even as he severed the binding around her wrists. Uncontrollable gasps jerked her chest. Her arms flopped as though belonging to someone else. She braced herself, but her hands sank into the squab, seemingly no longer attached to her. She drew them together and began rubbing them slowly, tenderly at first, then with purpose.

The pain began. Searing pain. Pain that promised exquisite

normality—eventually. Through it all, she watched Hāmuera. His face was pale, but determination shone from his eyes. The moment his hands were freed, he began rubbing them vigorously, and Alex realised he was working to restore circulation as quickly as possible too. Action would be futile before blood restored strength to arms and hands.

Travis was winding straps that had secured the cartons and was placing them in a small locker down by the stern. As he bent over the locker, Alex saw him covertly loosen the stern rope. The Asian had his back to him, and anyone looking down from the trawler would have merely seen Travis' back hunched over the locker. He picked up one end of the last strap and wound it into a tight circle, moving forward as he did so. As the tail of the strap lifted off the floor, he made for a locker near the wheel.

It was time for a distraction. But before she could think, Hāmuera let out an anguished cry and began shaking his hands as though stung by hornets. Although diverted but a brief moment, when Alex looked back, Travis gave her a quick nod. The for'ard holding rope had been loosened.

Hāmuera was a good actor. His pain seemed real. He clasped his hands between his knees. He pulled them out and rubbed them vigorously. Tears ran down his face.

The man was devoid of compassion. His face lit with pleasure.

Hāmuera extended his arms as if to show him the cause of his distress. Loud guffaws burst from the man.

It was his last laugh. In the later retelling, it seemed as though everything happened slowly and in order, not the chaotic brief seconds it took in reality.

As Hāmuera straightened, Alex instinctively fell on all fours behind the man. The shove when it came was powered by all the fury the young warrior could muster. The man stumbled backward and immediately toppled over Alex's crouched form. His legs draped across her briefly before sprawling sideways.

Instantly, Hāmuera was upon him. The heel of his palm pressed momentarily against the man's mouth before he drove it upwards in a savage path that ripped the man's top lip, split his nostrils either side of his bridge, exposing its gristle before leaving a flap of soggy eyelid against his temple.

The man bellowed a mixture of pain and fury. He flung his head from side to side to evade the bombardment of blows that followed. Hāmuera seemed unable to stop. His breath punctuated each blow with explosive grunts and hisses. Blood smeared the man's face and formed a dark pool beside his head.

Alex was paralysed by the fury of Hāmuera's attack, but Travis sprang to the ladder that swayed against the dark hull of the trawler, where the bulky form of Mr Liu was descending with remarkable agility and speed.

Travis met him just above the boat, and as one leg searched for the next rung, he grappled with it, attempting to pull him from his hold. Mr Liu clung limpet-like to the ladder. He managed to break the hold and kicked out viciously, grazing the side of Travis's head.

'Go, girl! Get going!' Travis yelled. 'Now!' Ignoring the pain and the ringing in his burning ear, he flung himself at the flailing leg again.

For an instant, Alex failed to grasp the instruction. It was the sight of Mr Liu's accomplice overpowering Hāmuera that stung her into action. She leapt over the bench seat, slamming into the captain's chair as she overbalanced. With one hand, she steadied herself by the chair while the other panicked for the throttle levers. Her hand met the metal T of the handles. She forced them hard forward.

The motors screamed, but nothing happened.

Hāmuera and the Asian were on their feet, the man scrabbling at his belt. Hāmuera dropped his shoulder and propelled himself into the man's stomach. To the side, she saw Mr Liu drop to the deck, where Travis had just sprawled. He reached for his handgun.

In that instant, Alex spotted the gear lever to the side of the wheel. She rammed it forward. The gears screeched hideously and thudded before the craft dug its stern into the water and lurched backward.

Alex almost lost her grip on the lever as her seat spun and tried to smash her into the instrument panel. The four bodies behind her tumbled forward and hurtled over the bench seat behind her. In greater panic, she fought to return the gear lever to neutral and the throttles to idle. *Forward gear, pull lever down!*

The two Asians struggled to their feet. Mr Liu had lost his handgun, but the bloodied face of his accomplice leered viciously over the pistol being levelled at Alex. Travis sprang to his feet and lunged at the gun.

Suddenly a mass of flailing limbs shot to the rear of the boat as Alex forced the gear lever and the throttles forward. The bow leapt and the boat careened along the side of the trawler before abruptly jerking around, throwing the stern outwards in a great churning of water.

Instinctively, Alex pulled back the throttles and gear lever. The stern line had slid clear, but the bow line had jammed. The next moment, Hāmuera was beside her.

'No more throttle!' he yelled. 'I'll clear the line!'

Alex glanced behind. The men were disentangling like rugby players from a collapsed scrum. The Asian was the first to his feet. He lumbered towards her like a wounded animal, bloodied, torn, and enraged.

'Now!' barked Hāmuera.

For the second time, the bow rose as the twin propellers tore at the water. The craft pranced ahead, freed from the rope. The Asian overbalanced and grabbed frantically for the rope ladder.

Once she had gained control of the boat, Alex looked fleetingly over her shoulder. The Asian swung by one hand above the twin propeller trails. Below him, two forms splashed in the shrinking circle of orange sea, Mr Liu and . . . Travis was gone too.

Something zipped past her.

'Shooting. Get down!' Hāmuera yelled.

Instantly, there was a metallic click and a ping that ricocheted into the dark. Two further flashes pricked from the dark waterline of the trawler, but already they had sped out of range of the pistol. Ahead, only the dark sea.

In the expansive freedom of the sea, they whooped and hollered. The wind that battered their faces and fiercely rippled their hair sucked out their tension. Spray smashed against the Perspex screen and spattered their faces. Their eyelashes tickled with droplets. They were alive. They were free. They laughed without restraint.

When the lights of the trawler were almost an imagining on the horizon, Alex drew the throttles back. The ride smoothed out, the wind lessened, and spray splashed sideways in looping slashes of white.

Hāmuera drew alongside, and placing one hand on her shoulder and the other over her hand on the throttle, he looked closely at her.

'You are something else, you know that?' he said. Even in the dim starlight, she saw the admiration in his eyes.

'Me? You've got to be kidding. *You're* the something else. All I did was get out of there as fast as I could. You . . .' She stopped, unsure of how to convey her feelings. Finally, in a halting voice, she said, 'You were awesome . . . like, fighting that brute and . . . he was going to shoot me. Thanks.' It seemed such a pathetic response.

His hand remained on her shoulder as he said, 'What? Shoot my girlfriend?' An unusual silence followed before he said, 'What sort of guy would do that anyway?'

The forward motion slowed as Alex brought the motors to idle and the gears into neutral. The bow levelled, and their wake caught up, giving rhythmic nudges ahead. Finally there was just the slop of water on the beam and the quiet pulsing of the motors.

'Which way to home?'

Hāmuera considered. He peered all around. There was nothing to give direction other than the compass on the instrument panel.

'Haven't a clue where we are.' He stooped to inspect a square blue-and-yellow display on the panel. 'Satnav,' he read out loud. It's one of those things that tell you where you are anywhere in the world—if you know how to read it,' he added, his voice indicating he couldn't.

Alex meanwhile had been quietly calculating. 'We need to head somewhere west.' Then with growing confidence, she continued, 'That's right. We had to be heading at least north or east out from the bay, so it'll be the reverse, won't it?'

'Good thinking, Alexandra.'

'We'll reach land heading west anyway, even if it's not the Bay of Islands.'

'Better than the other way. It's a long way to China.' Hāmuera snickered.

'Chile, more likely, and don't talk about China. I don't want to see another Chinese again.'

'Not Chinese, those men. Chinese don't fish in our waters. They're not Japanese either, so they must be Koreans.'

'Well, whatever they are, let's get as far away as possible from them. Let's go home. You drive.'

She released the controls over to Hāmuera, who tried to keep the boyish look off his face. Before he could move the throttles, the motors ran rough for a few seconds, raced, then died completely.

They looked at each other in mild alarm. Hāmuera twisted the ignition keys and ground the starter until it began to run slower. He slid off the captain's chair. When he returned, he said simply, 'Bullet nicked the fuel tank. We're out of juice.'

Chapter 18

Last Gasp

Every light blazed in the house. The front door was closed, but a pond of warm light poured through its glass panels on to the grass outside. Almost before Dan had brought his car to a sliding halt, Samuel leapt out. Fionna was on the telephone and was startled by the door bursting open. Immediate relief spread across her tense face.

'They've just arrived,' she said, her voice pitched high with excitement and relief. 'I'll get back to you soon.'

Replacing the receiver, her incredulous expression fixed on the boy for a moment before she exploded.

'Samuel, where on earth have you been? We've been worried sick! Your father is—'

She broke off in mid-sentence as Dan's frame filled the doorway. 'Oh, hello,' she said. 'I didn't realise . . . Did you find them and—'

Samuel ran around the kitchen bench to his mother. 'Mum, they've got Alex. We have to go after them. Where's Dad?' he implored.

'Who's got Alex? What are you saying?' Her eyes flicked from Samuel to Dan then back. 'Who's got Alex?' she repeated, her voice barely under control.

'We better call the police first,' Dan said, reaching across the bench to lift the telephone.

She stood transfixed, tearfully hugging Samuel as Dan spoke into the hand-piece, her eyes widening with each revelation. Samuel tried several times to speak to her, but she quickly silenced him, intent upon hearing every detail relayed to the police. When he had finished, she went straight to the intercom.

'Are you there, Greg?' She waited. 'Greg, can you hear me? Answer, please.' There was an edge of desperation in her voice.

'He's down at the bach,' she explained. 'We expected the children to turn up down there . . . if they were . . . I mean, if they . . . if they hadn't drowned.'

The last admission jerked from her chest amid released tears. She sank, trembling, to the floor beside the intercom and pressed and held the button that transmitted a call signal. The moment she lifted off, Greg's breathy voice came through.

'Sorry. I've been down at the beach. I only just heard you. Any news? Over.'

'Yes, Samuel's here, but Alex has been taken. Come up, Greg. I need you here. Over.'

'Taken? Where? Where is she?' Then processing the tone of her voice, he said, 'OK, I'm coming straight away.' The cable motor began almost immediately.

Dan stood the other side of the kitchen servery. A thick streak of dried blood ran from a congealed patch in his hair and blotched his collar tomato red. He looked faint.

'Come and sit down, Mr . . .' Fionna began.

'Dan,' he said. 'I'm Dan.'

'He tried to stop them taking us, Mum,' Samuel said, 'but they knocked him out.'

Dan sank into one of the armchairs. The ranch sliders, their glass blackened by the night, reflected dark images, scenes filtered through a portal from another hollow, unreal dimension. Like the events of the day.

'Any chance of some aspirin or something for this head of mine? I'm feeling it a bit,' Dan said, gingerly touching his head. He gently massaged his neck with both hands.

'Who's taken Alex? Where is she now?' Fionna's voice betrayed the hysteria forming like gas bubbles in boiling mud, barely below the surface, building in intensity, ready to burst through the surface without warning. She busied herself looking for a painkiller in the pantry.

'You heard me tell the police about the Korean fishing boat and pāua smuggling? They're probably on board that boat. The boss man we only know as Mr Liu. He found out the kids had seen what was happening. He wanted to take them with him. Unfortunately, I got put out of action when I tried to reason with him. This young fellow told me about what happened after that,' Dan said, smiling wanly and nodding at Samuel.

'You said "they". You mean Alex, don't you? Samuel's here,' Fionna said, handing over some soluble aspirin in a tumbler of water. Puzzlement briefly replaced anxiety.

'Hāmuera was there too, Mum,' Samuel interjected. 'We've got to find them. They had guns.'

Just then, Greg pushed through the door. In a glance, he took in Fionna, hands to her pale face, Samuel looking oddly bigger than usual, and the stranger with a blood streak down his head.

'OK, tell me where she is and if she's all right, then tell me how this has happened.'

In response, three voices tumbled over each other informing, describing, explaining, to the increasing concern of detective Gregory Armstrong. Finally, he went to the telephone.

'Police,' he said abruptly. There was a brief pause during which his eyes looked intently beyond their hollow reflections in the ranch slider. The next moment, his gaze shifted to the telephone as he gave a string of information and requests.

'Right,' he said, placing the receiver down, 'they're organising Search and Rescue for first light, and the navy are sending a patrol vessel up from Auckland as soon as it can be crewed. The local coast guard have also been alerted.'

He put his arms around Fionna and held her tight. 'There's nothing we can do. It's out of our hands now,' he whispered. 'Pray. That's about all we can do.'

Alex awakened, disorientated. Clouds had consumed the stars. A brisk wind had corralled the sea into uncomfortable lumps and rolls. She sat up, aware that she had been snug against Hāmuera, who was now stretching, grasping for consciousness. He yawned then suddenly became alert.

'You all right?' he asked. His voice sounded unpractised.

'A bit cool, that's all,' she replied.

'Cool? You're amazing, actually.'

'You know what I mean. Don't be silly,' Alex responded. The mild reprimand in her tone couldn't conceal her pleasure at the compliment.

He stood and rolled with the swell. 'No. I mean it. You got a lot of guts for a girl. The girls I know would have been crying and wanting their mothers or something, but you're not like that, eh.'

She balanced beside him in companionable silence. Somehow, each understood the other was processing events, exploring possibilities, considering actions.

Sea and sky were one dark mass, and without a horizon to view, after a while, Alex tasted the beginnings of motion sickness in her saliva.

Just my luck! The girl with guts gets to heave them over the side. Great! Now what will he think of me?

Suddenly, Hāmuera stiffened.

'What?' Alex asked, sensitive to the change in atmosphere.

'Over there, just to starboard of our stern.' He turned her by the shoulders. 'See?'

Alex searched the dark. 'What am I meant to be seeing?'

'Can't you see? Steaming lights. Red and green.' He took her chin and guided her face. 'You're looking too high. Down.' Almost instantly, she saw them, small but bright.

Over the next few minutes, the lights rose a little higher above their stern, growing steadily larger. She watched with increasing apprehension. Finally, Hāmuera said, 'Reckon we're pretty much in their path.'

'Is it them, do you think?' Alex found herself breathing rapidly.

'Didn't see any other boats out here, did we? Whether it's them or not, we gotta be ready. So . . .' His thoughts raced, but no clear plan would form. *Steaming lights. Green for starboard, red for port. Red for danger, green for good. Danger or good? Red for panic, green for calm. Think green about the red.*

Deep down drumming diesel in the dark. Without motors, they were powerless.

'They probably won't hit us, but if the worst does happen, stick with our boat. If we capsize, get back and cling on even if you can't get back on board,' he instructed.

His advice was sound, but it filled Alex with dread. Not even a faint glow from shore lights could be seen. They must be many kilometres from land. She knelt down and grasped the bench seat. The thought of being pitched into the black sea so far from everything strangled her courage. Perhaps she wouldn't find their boat again. What then? How long could she stay afloat? How long before her muscles and organs, sucked clear of warm blood, doomed her to death by drowning?

Dear God, You've got to help us. Please, dear God, don't let it happen.

Diesel engines reverberating. Steaming lights towering then disappearing abruptly overhead. A mass, blacker than the night, looming above.

A scream like a tormented gull escaped her mouth. She clung to her seat in mortal fear as it bucked and rolled in the solid wall of water punched aside by the ship's bow.

She was aware in the same moment of Hāmuera's scrambling, tumbling form sliding across the deck, and the massive hull continuously slicing past like a freight train over a rail crossing before, amazingly, the throbbing engines were behind them, the threshing propellers hissing at her.

'Hāmuera!' she called. 'Hāmuera, are you OK?'

There was no reply. Diesel engines rumbled a dull decrescendo. She focussed her eyes, trying to analyse the darkness in the tossing boat. She called again, but louder. Still no reply.

Please, God, let him be all right.

'Hāmuera!' This time, she screeched at full volume.

'Here.' Her fear became reality. The faint reply came from astern.

'Where? Call again!' she yelled, hoping to gain some idea of direction and distance on the water. This time, she gauged him to be about twenty metres behind and to her right. A strange calm descended upon her, and a clear picture of what she had to do flooded her brain. On all fours, she made her way to the aft locker, where Travis had coiled the ties. Tossing the ties aside, her rummaging hands felt two neatly coiled ropes.

'I'm throwing out some lines. Can you swim to them?' she yelled. She stood, carefully keeping her balance, and threw one as far as she could. It didn't seem to go far, but she tied it to a fixture anyway.

'Keep calling so I know where you are.' His voice was edgy.

'Cooee!' she called, remembering the bush call the Australian ranger had taught her. It should travel easier over water than in the bush. 'Cooee!'

'Good . . . I can hear.'

She imagined he was closer.

'I've thrown one. Can you find it?' He didn't answer immediately.

'Keep calling,' he said, and then amid some coughing and choking, he said, 'I'm swimming to you . . . a bit tired.'

'Here's the next one,' she shrilled. It snaked out, and a faint grey line scribed the water as it slapped across the surface.

'Can't see it . . . water's a bit rough.'

His voice sounded further away this time.

God, I know you can see the end from the beginning, but don't let this be his end. Please help him get back. Don't let him drown.

A heavy sensation settled over her at the thought of Hāmuera drowning and being washed up like that body at the lagoon.

'Cooee! Cooee!' Her calls came with renewed strength.

Wind tugged at her hair and rippled her clothes. The boat presented more surface to the wind than a body barely out of the water. He was falling further behind even though he was swimming.

It was a seriously flawed decision that followed and one that later Alex agreed was foolhardy. She scrabbled for the ties she had tossed on the floor, and passing one through panicking fingers, she found an end. She swiftly tied it around her waist, and the other end she clamped between her teeth.

In a moment, she was sliding into the water, ignoring the initial shock of cold. At once, she began to side crawl, her right arm swimming, her left hand keeping contact with one of the floating ropes.

She heard Hāmuera calling, more urgently this time, but she couldn't answer for fear of losing the tie end between her teeth. And then she found it—the end of the rope. With her left hand, she held it securely, and with her right hand, she removed the tie from her mouth. *Left over right and right over left.* The reef knot wouldn't slip. She let the rope go.

'Cooee!' she called, trying to lift her head above the waves. 'Hāmuera? Where are you?'

A wave slopped over her face, and the bite of salty water filled her throat and nose. She shook her head and wiped the stinging water from her eyes as her lungs fought for air.

'Alex . . . here!' His voice was to her left and not far away.

'Where? Keep talking.'

'Can't swim much . . . more.'

She heard his exhausted gasps faintly over the breaking waves. In the same moment, she caught sight of a dark blob on the crest of a swell.

'I can see you!' she shouted. 'Hold on, Hāmuera.'

She struck out in her practised freestyle, and as she rose on a swell, she saw him clearly in the trough below. He was struggling, his strength almost gone.

'I'm here. Hold on, Hāmuera.'

She swam down the swell, but he rose on the next and slid down the other side before she could reach him.

The next moment, Alex felt the tie pull firmly around her waist. She had reached the end of the line. So close but so far. Panic took possession of her. She lowered her head and threshed her arms and kicked her legs in desperation, not lifting for breath until her lungs began to siphon in water. And then he was there, just beyond reach.

'Can't come further . . . rope tight.' She gasped. 'Come on, help me . . . swim . . . here.'

His arms struggled to clear the surface. After four feeble attempts, he stopped. His head disappeared below the surface as they both slid into the next trough. As she mounted the next wave, Alex turned her head, searching desperately for him. And then she saw him. He was face down, but his feet kicked slowly and his arms languidly swept at the water.

Please, dear God. The wave lifted, and the next moment, her fingers touched clothing. *Thank you, thank you.* She wasn't going to let go now. She grasped the material and hauled on it. His pale face broke the surface as a wave slid under them. He gasped for air and gagged on the water that flooded his throat.

'Hold my belt. Can you hear me, Hāmuera? Hold my belt,' she implored. His hands groped for her waist and latched weakly onto the waistband of her shorts. 'Just hold on. Don't try to swim, OK? I'll do the work.'

Hāmuera didn't answer, but she sensed his concession, for his grip remained on her waistband and his body floated out behind. She began pulling the two of them, hand over hand along the tie and then the rope, back towards their boat.

After the initial shock, the water had seemed warm, but her hands had become fumbling cold and spasms gripped her stomach. Once, she lost her grip on the rope and, for a terrifying moment, floundered to regain it. After silently reprimanding herself, she concentrated fiercely. Her own strength was waning. She doubted she would have had strength to reach the boat without the rope. Hāmuera definitely wouldn't. He depended on her.

The boat was a ghostly form above her, the outboard motors projecting like horns of some weird aquatic animal, when Hāmuera lost his grip.

Chapter 19

Adrift

The radio weaved its way into Samuel's dream. He was captain of a deep-sea fishing launch calling other craft in his adventure fishing company. The sea boiled with terror as marlin rounded up a school of fish. The UHF radio cackled with excited voices as the fleet raced to join him. Mr Liu entered the cabin, demanding a lure for his rod, but suddenly, the rod became a gun. Mr Liu tried to grab him, but Samuel began running for his life over the water, not touching it, stretching, lifting, willing every part of his body to lift off and fly.

The arch of one foot began to cramp, and instantly, the dream vanished, leaving a faint imprint on his brain as he curled his toes, stretched, and yawned.

Someone had the radio on quite loud: 'And the prime minister said today that the International Whaling Commission had not conveyed how strongly New Zealand objects to Japanese whaling in the southern oceans. Their continuing justifications on the grounds of scientific research will be seen for the sham that it is. New Zealand has strict quotas on international fishing in its economic zone, which exclude any aquatic mammals from both commercial and recreational fishers. He said that there are harsh penalties for both commercial and recreational fishers who deliberately ignore limitations on fish and shellfish in our territorial waters and that the international community should . . .'

They had stayed in the house overnight, sleeping on top of the beds already prepared for Gran and Grandpa, hoping for the telephone call that would tell them Alex was safe and on her way home. Samuel quickly sat up. Alex. Hāmuera. Had they been found yet?

Greg stood beside the servery, his ear inclined to the radio despite its volume. A plume of steam from the kettle, illuminated by early morning rays, seemed to rise from the top of his head. Fionna was busy setting cutlery and plates on the table as Samuel padded across the floor.

'Have they found—'

Dad cut him short with a gesture. 'Listen!'

'And police say marijuana will be hitting the streets of our main cities in greater quantities because of the favourable growing conditions over many parts of the country unless more resources are made available for helicopter and fixed-wing aerial surveillance. And that's the news. In a moment, the weather.'

'Nothing then,' Fionna said. She looked grey and drawn.

'It's only six thirty. Don't expect too much,' Greg replied, switching the radio off. 'A plane should be in the air about now. They'll find her. Don't you worry about that. They can't have gone too far.' His voice sounded surer than the look on his face.

'I know where it is, Dad,' Samuel volunteered.

'Where what is, son?' Greg said absently.

'Our marig . . . our marijuana.'

'What?'

'Our marijuana. It's in that big barn on the farm, where the pāua was. It's in a thing hanging down from the roof. I saw it.'

Greg and Fionna looked at each other with slightly raised eyebrows. Finally, Greg said, 'You sure saw a lot yesterday, didn't you? Mum and I are very proud of what you did, Samuel. You were very brave and very grown-up. You did everything just right.'

'Gee, thanks, Dad. I really appreciate you saying that.' His parents turned to hide their smiles. Sometimes he seemed mature beyond his years.

Dan emerged, looking crumpled and obviously suffering a headache again. Before anyone could speak, the telephone jangled. Greg pounced on it.

'Greg here.' A slight gap. 'Yes, certainly, thanks.'

Over the next few minutes, he mainly listened.

'That was the search centre,' he said as he returned the receiver. 'They're keeping us informed of any developments. A Cessna has just taken off from Kerikeri, and the coast guard have one boat near the cape and another near Marsden Cross, waiting for directions. The navy boat is off Tutukaka, heading north. They've picked up several craft on their radar. It's all happening. She'll be right.'

He enveloped Fionna in his arms. 'She'll be right,' he replied. 'No need to cry. Come on, love. We've got someone above on our side. He'll watch out for her.'

'And Hāmuera, my friend. Don't forget him,' said Samuel.

Alex hadn't realised she had slept. It seemed her mind had not shut down, but with a jerk, she awoke. Her arms were still wrapped around Hāmuera as when she had fallen asleep. She had hugged him partly out of thankfulness, but mainly so they could both gain warmth and stop the incessant shivering that jagged at their muscles and rippled uncontrollably through their bodies. The small shade cover she had draped over them, though made of a heavy plastic with no warmth in itself, had protected them from the wind. For several minutes, she lay not moving, listening for his breathing. She felt it rather than heard it: a slow, shallow expanding of his chest. He was alive, thank God.

The chaotic and terrifying moments after Hāmuera had let go of her waistband surged uninvited into her mind. He had been barely conscious when she had grabbed his shirt again. He had tried to help her, but his feeble attempts had little effect. She had released her own hold on the rope to find him, and the boat had slowly moved away from them. Her own efforts had become weaker, and with Hāmuera's weight, she had become frantic to get back to the boat.

The thing that slid across her face at first made her lash out in fear until she realised it was the first rope she had thrown to Hāmuera. It hadn't been useful before, but how providential it had then become. With it, she had managed to haul them both to the stern. She had swallowed a lot of water while somehow passing the rope under his arms and tying it around his chest.

When finally she had lumbered with leaden limbs up the short stern ladder, she had kept the rope as taut as she could to keep his head clear of the water. Heaving on the rope did little to lift Hāmuera on board. She coaxed, she yelled, she threatened, she promised, she bullied until he tried again. Just how she had got him up the steps was unclear, but she remembered the exhilaration and exhaustion that wrenched bolts of laughter mingled with sobs from her as they both flopped there, sodden, shivering, and alive.

Alex pushed the cover to one side and sat up. The morning sun rocked over and off them with the sea's motion. By the height of the sun, she reckoned it must be about seven o'clock. She stood and surveyed the horizon. The air was morning-fresh clear. No wind. No boats. No land. Nothing.

Hāmuera lay motionless. Salt-sticky hair serrated his pale face. Closed eyelids, thin and etched with crimson, covered his eyes like drapes above the slack blue lines of his lips. If she hadn't felt him breathing, she would have thought him dead. She shuddered for both the thoughts of their fortunate escape and the coolness of the morning. A thorough search of the lockers and several cupboards provided some bottled water, a first-aid kit, bright yellow foul-weather jackets and trousers, and emergency flares in a sealed yellow container, but no food.

Her body felt strangely heavy, and every joint and muscle ached as she struggled into a pair of trousers. They were far too big, as was the jacket, but after rolling up arm and leg lengths, she felt much warmer.

She sat in the captain's chair. The instrument panel stared blankly at her. A swig of bottled water loosed her tongue from the salty roof of her mouth. She peered ahead then revolved the chair to face the stern. The horizon scribed its curve against the sky, but the harder she searched, the more her eyes watered. Wiping them proved unhelpful. Caked salt from eyelids and cheeks stung them into welling ponds. After flushing them clean with several splashes of water, she scanned the ocean again.

The vast expanse pushed to the horizon, unbroken except for a distant dull smudge off to port. A wave of excitement began to grip her stomach. She stood on the bench seat and tried to make out a shape, but with the motion of the sea and at that distance, it was difficult to be sure. But it had to be a boat, surely. It was unlikely the trawler would have waited around for daylight, especially inside territorial waters and with the likelihood of a search having begun. She continued interrogating the shape, willing it to be a boat. Twice she surveyed the sea in the hope of seeing another, a closer, more definite sighting. When on the second occasion she could not immediately find it again, a mild panic began. Once she located it again, she determined to not let her eyes move off it.

After some time of willing it to come closer, Alex felt a pang of disappointment, for it had now moved to starboard and was definitely becoming more distant. Her downcast eyes met the deck, where the emergency flares lay. Hope rebounded. Of course! Flares would attract attention.

The lid unscrewed easily. Tipping the contents onto the deck, she discovered two identical orange tubes with 'Parachute flare' printed in bold lettering on their sides. She selected one, and following the instructions and line drawings on the side, she unscrewed the bottom plug to allow the pull cord to fall out. Then holding the tube above her head, she braced her legs and pulled sharply downwards on the cord.

The detonation was louder than expected. The flare rocketed skywards, trailing white smoke in an arc that ceased moments before a bright ball burst in an intense red blaze. Although the casing was hot, she barely noticed it, marvelling at the red star suspended against a pale blue sky.

'Don't shoot, man. I surrender.' Hāmuera's voice was weak.

Alex started for a moment at the sound of his voice, then elation welled up. His humour hadn't drowned.

'You're awake.'

''Course I am. What do you expect with all that racket, eh?'

'How are you feeling?'

He pushed himself gingerly into a sitting position and rubbed his head with both hands. Several times, he began to speak before flopping down again.

'I'm feeling lucky to be alive, that's what,' he said softly. 'I nearly drowned.'

Alex said nothing and pretended not to notice the tears gathering in the corners of his eyes.

'I saw you, in the water,' he continued. 'I was pretty much a goner, but you gave me something to swim for. Thanks.'

'You want some water?' she said, trying to prevent her own tears from filling any silence. 'Or have you had enough to drink?' she added, surprised at her own attempt at humour.

A smile twisted his mouth as he reached a hand out. She gave him the bottle then stood to watch the flare, low on its descent towards the sea. Scanning the horizon, she spied no response to her distress signal. And no dark smudge. She sat down beside Hāmuera.

'No one around. I'll save the last one for night-time.' The full meaning of what she said suddenly dawned on her. They could be out there all day. She felt rather than heard her stomach rumble.

'Hope you're not hungry,' she said. 'There's nothing to eat. Plenty of water though.' Then she busied herself trying to work out how the shade cloth could attach to the tubular frame that pulled back from over the windscreen. The morning sun already had a bite to it and she had removed the trousers and jacket. Their skin would need some protection.

'That was Mum,' Greg said, replacing the receiver. 'They're just leaving now. And they've got her cousin, Daya, with them as a surprise for Alex. I didn't tell them about . . . things. By the time they arrive, we could have

Alex back, or at least know she's all right. Didn't want to worry them. Dad drives fast enough as it is.'

Fionna nodded. 'Yes, New Year's Eve traffic will slow them down. She'll be back by then. I just wish I knew what's happening.' There was a keening tone in her voice.

'Nearly nine o'clock. The plane should spot them any time soon. A trawler can't get away that quickly. Once they're spotted, the navy will get to them pretty quickly. Then it's just a matter of finding out if they're on board or . . .' Greg's voice trailed off.

Fionna bit her lip and went quickly through the open ranch slider to stand on the grass, where she pretended to look out to the distant islands. Tears blurred her vision and slid down each cheek. Samuel sensed his mother's grief and joined her. He slipped an arm around her waist.

'She's going to be fine, Mum. God's got it all sussed.' He looked up at her with such an intense confidence that Fionna had to smile.

'I know, Samuel. I'm just a bit tired, that's all. You're a good boy.' She hugged him closely. 'Now why don't you go down and see if the fish are biting at the beach.'

'Call me as soon as she's been found, Mum,' he said as he eagerly complied with her suggestion.

Greg came out into the sun, a steaming cup in each hand. 'Time for a cuppa,' he said kindly. The phone jangled inside.

'I'll get it!' She left Greg standing, cup in each hand, and bounded to the phone. 'Hello, Fionna speaking.'

Greg joined her, trying to read her face as she listened intently. Her facial messages were conflicting.

'Thank you, thank you so much. We truly appreciate being kept informed. Goodbye.'

'What?' Greg pumped.

'The navy located two trawlers, and the first one they boarded is the one. They found the two men Samuel talked about because they were dressed in civilian clothes. They found Dan's mate locked up, and he's told them about Alex and that Māori boy.' She looked a little confused as she said, 'They're not on board. They think they escaped in the boat that took them out to the trawler. I don't understand.'

Dan appeared. 'I heard all that. They must be pretty gutsy kids. The good news is there's easily enough fuel on board to get them back—if they can navigate, that is. They won't be able to see land from that far out, but—'

'Dad.' Samuel's voice startled them. Hearing the phone ring as he was about to go down the track, he had returned. 'Alex and Hāmuera will take that boat back to the farm. We can go in the runabout and I'll show you where it all happened and you can see the marijuana. Then I can get our dinghy and row it back. I can do it on my own. I'm a really good rower, better than Alex. OK, Dad?' His parents looked at each other.

'OK, then,' Dad consented. 'It will be over to Russell police to decide on who does the scene examination, but I'll give the place a look over and seal it off. No harm in that, I guess.'

No second invitation required, Samuel was waiting at the top of the track as his father appeared with Dan in tow.

'I can beat the train down, Dad,' he said.

'I bet you can.' Greg smiled as he settled Dan into the upper seat. 'You get the life jackets for us, and we'll meet you on the beach. Go!'

The motor rattled, and Samuel set off like a sandhopper evading a wave.

The sound was faint. Hāmuera was standing beside her now, feet apart, balancing with difficulty in the rolling swell that had built up over the morning. Clouds had begun to stretch over the horizon to port, and Alex silently considered that was where land lay, hopefully not too far from the Bay of Islands. The sky all about them was clear blue, however, and their searching eyes tried to pick out the shape of an aircraft. The engine grew louder.

'There it is,' Hāmuera exclaimed, pointing.

Alex could see nothing. 'Where? Show me.'

'It's not that high. Lower. Look along my arm. See?'

She put her head on his upper arm and tried sighting along it, but the motion of the sea kept jostling them apart. He slipped an arm around her waist and drew her in front of him. Then holding her firmly to him with the free arm, he said, 'Try now.'

Alex sensed Hāmuera's closeness. It was different from the night when she had wrapped her arms around him for mutual warmth. Now she sensed his vitality, thrilled at his closeness. Her eyes found the small dark dot of the aircraft, distant and lower to the horizon than she had been looking.

'The flare!' Hāmuera pulled away from her. 'They can't see us. Too far away. They'll see a flare though.'

'No, not yet,' Alex objected. 'It's the last one. Save it for night-time.'

But Hāmuera ignored her. He scrabbled with the container and soon had the tube in his hand. As the flare traced skywards, Alex felt affection draining. Anger took its place.

'That's right!' she railed. 'Don't listen to me. I put my life on the line for you, and you don't trust me. If they don't see it, we're sunk. Happy now?' She dumped herself on the bench seat with her back to him, hiding tears of indignation.

Hāmuera looked crestfallen. 'I just thought if the plane was there, it was worth the chance.'

'Well, you didn't think, did you.'

Hāmuera decided against replying. Instead, he watched the flare slowly drop into the sea. Then shifting his gaze, he watched the hovering dot of the aeroplane recede and finally disappear.

Above them, the noon sun burned. Around them, the unending sea ridged and rolled. Within them, isolated by their emotions, unable to talk, unable to apologise or accept an apology, hurt wedged between them.

A cluster of vaguely inquisitive faces, gilded by the late afternoon sun, lined the side of the vehicular ferry leaving for Ōkiato Point. A police car and a four-wheel drive, emblazoned with police stripes, straddled Ōpua wharf. A police officer sat in the car, and three others talked in a casual gathering to one side, occasionally looking beyond the yacht masts serenely rocking on their mooring lines.

The woman constable called from the car window, and the men gathered around her before moving as one to the 4 × 4 and driving towards the end of the wharf. The harbour master's assistant appeared from the office and followed on foot, carrying a satchel and clipboard.

Around the headland slunk the unmistakable shape of a trawler. Close behind it, less visible in battle grey yet bristling with authority, a naval patrol vessel escorted it towards the wharf.

Greg eased the throttle to neutral and turned the ignition off. The runabout slipped, silvery quiet, towards the sand. Climbing eagerly over the windscreen and kneeling on all fours, Samuel prepared to jump in and prevent the bow grating. Greg began raising the motor, and giving the signal to Samuel, he looked back and noticed Dan hunched near the stern.

'You OK? How's the head?' he asked.

Dan shook his head and looked rueful. 'It's OK. Just thinking about things.'

The bow touched the sand despite Samuel's efforts. 'That's OK, Sam. Just hold it there.'

A rope soon tethered the craft, and the three walked up the nearby ramp, eyes fixed on the large doors. They were wide open and not locked this time. Light flooded in, revealing the tractor and forlorn trailer standing alone on the concrete strip.

Samuel excitedly showed his father where his sister and Hāmuera had been held, then clambered up the hay bales to demonstrate where he had hidden. Dan lingered near the tractor.

'Now you can see the marijuana, Dad. Come on. It's through here,' Samuel shrilled.

They followed him through the wall of hay bales. There was sufficient light to see the frame with its contents held aloft. Greg pursed his lips and began a thorough visual examination of the scene before walking over to the chiller room. Using a handkerchief, he opened its door and peered inside for some time before grunting and shutting it firmly. Dan sidled up to him.

'You've gotta believe me about this. Travis and me were just the delivery boys. We had no idea about marijuana or kids being involved. We were just doing a job, earning some dough. We're no crims. We were just taking the stuff out there. I won't get prison for this, will I?'

'Tell the truth, no messing around, and I'll make sure you get the best deal,' Greg responded. 'At the moment you are an accomplice to exceeding limits and illegal exporting of pāua.'

Dan looked sombre.

'But not party to threatening to kill or kidnapping,' Greg continued. 'In fact, it's clear you attempted to prevent the kidnapping. You stood up to them and got your head bashed in for it. I think any judge would take that into account. Probably wipe out the earlier offences, if you haven't got any prior convictions.'

Dan looked happier. 'Couldn't see kids get involved, could I? Got four of me own.'

The rear door was not locked either. Greg eased his body through. The Mercedes sat contentedly where it had been left in the shade of the poplar trees and a huge pōhutukawa. He noted down the licence plate numbers.

'I'll get a trace on these. Could be interesting,' he muttered. He called to the others, 'Come out this way. I'll see if I can secure everything here, and I'll join you at the boat, Dan.'

Then turning to Samuel, he gave him the go-ahead to row the dinghy back. Samuel scampered away before the sentence was finished.

'I'm sorry for getting, you know, silly about the flare. I guess everything got to me a bit.'

Alex was holding a steaming cup of sweet tea in both hands, looking down at her feet, not daring to let Hāmuera see into her eyes. Someone told her that eyes are the window to the soul. It was true. Eyes give you away. They tell more than words.

Hāmuera said nothing.

After a moment, Alex spoke again. 'I shouldn't have hit you. I'm really, really sorry.'

Hāmuera still said nothing.

'Those things I said about you being a Māori and all that—I didn't mean them either. I don't even believe it, actually. I don't know why I said it. It's unforgivable, but . . . I'd really like you to try. Please, Hāmuera.' And when he still said nothing she added another 'Please'.

'Hey, we're on the news!' Hāmuera slipped the headphones from his ears so they clung to his neck. 'They just said about the navy taking a trawler into Ōpua and that the two kidnapped kids were brought back on a coast guard launch. Hey, we're famous!'

His dark eyes glittered, and tugging the headphones from his neck, he stepped partly up the companionway and called to the coast guard skipper, 'We're on the news. They say we're heroes.'

The skipper laughed back. ''Course you are. Foiled the smugglers, didn't you? You're outrageous you are, the pair of you.'

With the sleeve of the borrowed jersey, Alex smeared the tears that threatened to betray her. 'Really? What did they say? Tell me everything they said, I mean, *everything*.'

Hāmuera gave her an account of the radio item which, embellished in Hāmuera's typical style, had them both laughing insanely and retelling events far longer than they realised. The skipper interrupted to tell them they were approaching Clendon Point.

They raced up the companionway. Jack-and-Jill beaches linked arms to the left of the familiar headland. The point reached out to meet them, ochre and red scars from recent slips picked out in the late afternoon sun like road signs. Barely visible to their right, nestled in among an irregular green shadow of trees at the far end of Manawaora Bay, they glimpsed the outline of the building. An involuntary shudder rippled down Alex's spine.

She sensed Hāmuera's closeness and deliberately draped an arm over his shoulders. He responded with an arm around her waist and a broad smile.

'Bet you won't do this with your parents around, eh,' he said.

'You want a bet?'

They stood silently as Clendon Cove came into view. The diesel engines set to idle, and their forward motion slowed. The skipper called to Hāmuera to stand ready to put the engine into reverse when he dropped the anchor.

'Better not me, eh, Skip. Alexandra is better than me at that sort of thing.'

He pushed at Alex. 'Go on. I'll help let the anchor down—you know, men's work.' He winked mischievously at her.

Entering the wheelhouse, she took a quick lesson from the skipper and waited as the two men loosed the anchor chain. At the command, she gave a brief burst of reverse before shifting back to neutral. Soon the skipper returned.

'Good stuff,' he said. 'You can crew for me any day. You'd better get ready for the landing party now. Have you seen them?'

Alex stepped out of the wheelhouse. Dad's runabout was approaching fast.

'Mum! Dad! Oh, it's Gran and Grandpa too,' she squealed jumping up and down.

The dinghy was some distance back, and she spied Samuel straining at the oars. Someone vaguely familiar sat in the stern, waving. Then with sudden realisation, she shrieked, 'And that's Daya in the dinghy with Samuel. Oh man, is she going to be freaked out by this.'

'Hey, what's going on? That's my aunty and my nana too,' Hāmuera shouted. 'What are they all doing here?'

'They're in the same boat,' Alex said, stating the obvious. Then as if by sudden revelation, she repeated with more emphasis, 'They're all in the same boat, Hāmuera. We all are.'

Almost simultaneously, the diesel motor and the runabout engine stopped. For a moment, life hung suspended. Above the slapping of the water, the crackling of a million cicadas rattled the air. She looked at Hāmuera, and she knew he understood.

Glossary

Bach	Cabin or hut (originally from 'bachelor's dwelling'?)
Ehōa	(Māori) friend
Cicada	*Cicadoidea*—a summer flying insect that makes a loud daytime rasping noise using timbals in its abdomen
Gidday	(Colloquial Australasian) also 'g'day', a greeting, 'good day'
Haka	(Māori) a posture dance—for ceremonial or warfare effects
Ka pai	(Māori) good
Kahawai	(Māori) an edible coastal schooling fish
Kai	(Māori) food
Kai moana	(Māori) seafood
Kānuka	White tea tree, *Kunzea ericoides*—tall hardwood tree
Karakia	(Māori) a ritual chant, a prayer
Kawa-kawa	(Māori) *Macropiper excelsum*—small, densely branched pepper tree, with heart-shaped leaves
Kōrerō	(Māori) talk, discussion
Korowai	(Māori) flax cloak ornamented with black twisted tags or dog hair thrums. Usually a sign of high social position
Kowhai	(Māori) *Sophora*—native tree with hanging clusters of large yellow flowers in early spring
Mana	(Māori) prestige, personal supernatural force
Mānuka	Common tea tree, *Leptospermum scoparium*—scrub bush
Māori	Native people of NZ
Mere	(Māori) a short, flat weapon of stone, often of greenstone
Mozzies	(Colloquial Australasian) mosquitoes
Pākehā	(Māori) foreigner—originally referred to Europeans

Pipi	(Māori) *Paphies australis*—a common edible bivalve shellfish found in sandy mudflats at low tide
Pōhutukawa	(Māori) *Metrosideros excelsa*, 'NZ Christmas tree', named for its large red flowers that appear from December onwards
Ponga	(Māori)Tall silver tree fern, *Cyathea dealbata*—unique black trunk
Pūriri	Large spreading tree, *Vitex lucens*—smooth-barked limbs
Runabout	Open cockpit sea craft powered by outboard motor(s)
Transom	Upright section at the stern of a sea craft
Utu	(Māori) revenge

CPSIA information can be obtained
at www.ICGtesting.com
Printed in the USA
LVHW091343100222
710659LV00038B/489/J

9 781664 107496